MW01204984

ESCAPING PROPHECY
and Other Stories

Escaping Prophecy and Other Stories
by Cat Greenberg

Copyright ©2019 Mountain Cat Media LLC
Female of the Species ©1990
Lessons in the Dark ©1992
Power Play ©1994
All Rights Reserved

Published in the United States
by Mountain Cat Media LLC
www.mountaincatmedia.com

ISBN-9780-692-03353-1

Printed in the United States

Cover Art by:
Karen Rennaux

This book is a work of fiction. All characters,
names, locations, and events portrayed in this
book are fictional, and any resemblance to any
real people, situations, or incidents are purely
coincidental .

No part of this document may be reproduced or
transmitted in any form, by any means
(electronic, photocopying, recording, or
otherwise) without the prior written permission
of the publisher.

Contents

This book is dedicated to:
Bari Greenberg, the love of my
life, and forever my muse;
to my children
Aidan, Matthew and Valerie,
may you always keep your
sense of wonder;
and gratefully to Judy DaPolito,
teacher extraordinaire, whose
guidance and encouragement
brought my inner writer out.

A note from the Author

Thank you so much for letting me share my imagination with you. This anthology contains fourteen stories in total. For ten of them, this is the first printing. Of the four that are reprints, three are as they appeared in *Sword & Sorceress XI* and *Marion Zimmer Bradley's Fantasy Magazine*. The fourth is a major rewrite of a story that first appeared in the very limited publication of a small convention's program book. Why reprint them here? First, because I like them and want to give them a chance to find a new audience. Second, because I want my current name on them.

Before I was Cat Greenberg, I was Sandra Morrese—previous marriage, previous life, and a name I no longer want on my fiction. In a way, I reinvented myself after my divorce. More accurately, I finally got to know aspects of myself that I hadn't realized I'd suppressed for years. I started using Cat (derived from my middle name) more often than Sandra. In addition to fiction, I started a nonfiction project and began writing songs with my friend Bari Greenberg as I became more involved in filk* music. He had lost his wife to cancer, and we were both dealing with single-and-not-by-choice and would talk for hours. Eventually that friendship blossomed into love, and we were married. And so I bring these stories back with their proper authorship—Cat Greenberg, who I am today.

Bari Greenberg, in addition to being my wonderful life partner for far too brief a time, coauthored the story that gives this anthology its name, a stand-alone story that adds to our version of the fate of Kassandra of Troy from *Plausible Deniability,* which appeared in *Sword & Sorceress 29*, still available on Amazon from Marion Zimmer Bradley Literary Works Trust. I am very pleased to be able to give Bari this additional small bit of paper immortality. He was a talented budding author, and we had an enormous amount of fun writing Kassandra's story.

So without further ado, I give you *Escaping Prophecy.*

*"a musical culture, genre, and community tied to science fiction/fantasy/horror fandom" Source: Wikipedia.org (please check it out, good explanation.)

ESCAPING PROPHECY

by
Cat and Bari Greenberg

If you read our story "Plausible Deniability" (still in print in Sword & Sorceress 29*), then the main character will be familiar to you. If not, no worries, this is a stand alone story. It continues our version of the fate of Princess Kassandra, daughter of King Priam of Troy, a priestess of Apollo with the gift of prophecy, cursed by the god to see true but never be believed.*

I'm not dead, Kassandra mused. *I saw myself murdered. Gruesomely. Yet here I am, walking along the north road out of Mycenae.*

And I'm not *dead.*

Granted, history would say differently. Queen Clytemnestra had declared her dead after staying her hand; then she banished Kassandra, as she renamed her Eurayle. Kassandra shook her head. History really was subjective, written by the powerful. It could be wrong. It could even lie.

But was it a lie? In so many ways Kassandra had died, many times over. She'd died when her beloved Troia fell; died when her family was slain; died every time Agamemnon raped her; died when he dragged her back to Greece to be his concubine. If only they had listened to her . . . a useless line of thought. Of course, they hadn't; Apollo had seen to that the day she'd refused his bed.

So let Kassandra die a final time, she thought, and Eurayle be born. She certainly had nothing to lose. Everything she ever used to be or have was gone. It was an odd name to her ears, an Achaean name, but it would do.

Kassandra came out of her reverie, suddenly aware that the clamor of the day was now an eerie hush. The road, at first busy with travelers, was nearly deserted, and her contemplative stroll had let the caravan she'd been following pass long out of sight. The sun was getting low, and she was tired, hungry, and thirsty. Could she afford to rest? Where was she going to sleep? Nervously, she increased her pace.

Olive orchards and rows of grape vines filled either side of the road. Pondering the morality of taking a few barely ripe fruit, she stopped when an odd sound reached her. It was a crying child, but where? She saw no children anywhere about. A breeze through tangled branches scattered the sound. She stood very still, waiting for a pause so she could discern the direction—in the orchard, to the right.

The trees cast deep shadows in the dusk. She reflexively began a prayer, then decided to leave the gods out of this. She stepped into the orchard from the now empty road and called: "Hello? Do you need help?"

She'd gotten four rows in when a very small voice answered between sobs.

"I'm . . . I'm up . . . here." A distraught little boy of four or five perched in the twisted branches of an unusually large olive tree.

"I'm stuck and it hurts and," he said, tears streaming down, "and I want my Mama."

"It's all right," Kassandra said, "I'll help you. I was pretty good at climbing trees at your age. How did you get stuck?"

"My foot slipped, and I can't get it out."

"Don't pull on it," she warned. Her brother broke an ankle that way when they were seven. "I'll come up."

Kassandra dropped the cloak and sighed. She was not dressed for climbing trees. She pulled and tucked her skirt as best she could. Gripping the lowest branch where the trunk split, she hauled herself up, placing her feet carefully to avoid a similar fate as the child.

"My name is Ka—Eurayle," she said, continuing to talk to the boy.

"I'm Galenos. I'm almost five years old."

She smiled at the childish pride and sudden change of subject, now that his rescue was at hand. Three more branches, and she was beside him.

"Nice to meet you, Galenos."

"You talk pretty," he said. "Where are

you from?"

She paused. "A long way from here." She changed the subject before it got complicated. "Let's see about your foot."

His leg disappeared inside a crevice where two thick branches twined around each other. It was too dim to see, so she reached in and gently felt the shape of his foot and the crevice interior. "Don't pull until I tell you, Galenos, then pull very slowly."

Galenos sniffed and nodded.

It took some maneuvering to back his foot out through the twisting bark, but they managed. Kassandra climbed down first, then helped Galenos.

"Ow!"

She felt his ankle. It was twisted and swelling but thankfully not broken.

"I'll carry you."

After retrieving her cloak and securing it, she picked up Galenos.

"Now, let's find your mama and papa. Any idea where they are?"

"Papa is the caravan master. We're going to Arkadia for Philon's dedication at Hermes' temple. He's my big brother."

"You camp each night, right?"

"Uh-huh."

"Then, if we follow the road, we should be able to find them. They can't be too far ahead."

"Thank you for helping me," he said and hugged her neck. After all the evil that had befallen her since the Achaean army breached Troia's walls, she had forgotten there were still good things in the world, like a child's heartfelt gratitude. A simple act, yet it filled her with such joy, tears threatened.

A nearly full moon was rising, giving enough soft illumination to find the road again. She decided to hoist Galenos onto her shoulders. She'd have to be careful to avoid pulling on the injured ankle, but it made his weight easier to manage.

Galenos chatted about his father, Kosmas, and mother, Charis; his Gigia Sophia, who was Kosmas's mother; his sister Olina, three years older than he was; baby sister Eirene, who was just two; and his uncle, Phaidros, a smith who had been forced into service during the war.

"Papa hadn't seen Uncle Phaidros in ten whole years! He'd never got to see me, and Philon was just barely born when they made him leave. Mama says Hermes smiled on us, since we were in Mycenae when his ship arrived."

Phaidros had brought a soldier friend with him named Linos. "He doesn't talk much. I think he's sad."

Then there was Sophus, an artificer who often traveled with his father.

"His wife died last year. So he brought Auxentios and Bion with him. They're twins, a year older than me."

They'd been playing hide and seek together in the orchard. Galenos hid in the tree, and by the time he realized he was stuck, the others had already run too far ahead to hear him call.

Lastly, there was a scholar named Georgios and his wife, Tessa, returning to Elis with them. "Her belly's big 'cause she's going to have a baby."

After about an hour, Kassandra pointed ahead at two bobbing lights. "Look, I think they're searching for you."

The distance closed until the faces of two men and a woman scanning both roadsides by torchlight could just be made out.

Galenos shouted, "Mama! Papa!"

The woman closed the gap at a run.

"Galenos!"

Kassandra happily passed her burden over. "Be careful of his foot."

"Where were you?" The woman asked, trying to look him over and hug him at the same time.

"I got stuck in a tree and hurt my ankle. Eurayle got me down. But it still hurts."

"He twisted it badly," Kassandra said quietly, knowing her Luwian accent would sound foreign. "He won't be able to walk on it for a few days, and it should be wrapped for support, but I don't think it's broken."

By this time the men had caught up.

"My gratitude to you for helping my son," said the man who must have been Kosmas. "Please join us and let us thank you properly."

"I would be honored," Kassandra said, amazed at their welcome.

The five men gathered around the watch fire, the four women around the one they'd used for cooking. Children wandered from one group to the other. Kassandra sat finishing the simple stew and flat bread Charis had given her.

Whether because of her hunger or her circumstances, it seemed the most delicious meal she'd ever tasted.

Soon the women were discussing the futility of the war. She listened as they vilified Helen for being unfaithful, King Menelaus for not simply choosing another queen, and the flaws of prideful kings who used any excuse to gain glory in battle. They clearly thought such pursuits pointlessly wasteful.

Kassandra considered telling them the truth, how Paris caused the war through his foolish choice of Aphrodite's apple to possess Helen. Kassandra often wondered what might have happened if Paris had chosen Athena. Would the goddess really have given him the promised wisdom? Perhaps, but she had learned that the enticing flowers of godly gifts often held nasty thorns.

"You're very quiet, Eurayle," Charis said, collecting the bowl Kassandra had thoroughly cleaned. "But I see you like my cooking."

"It was wonderful. Thank you."

"You're most welcome," she said, sitting down next to her. "I am grateful you heard my son's cries and were kind enough to stop and help him. He was so far back, I fear we would not have found him."

"He's a charming boy," Kassandra said.

Charis chuckled. "Yes, he's much like his father."

"Where is he?"

"In our cart. He fell asleep right after he ate."

The two women sat quietly, then Charis asked, "Where are you going, Eurayle? You have no pack, no bedroll. Just a fine travel cloak over what appears to be an even finer gown. Forgive me, but you are not fit for the road."

Kassandra laughed a bit at the understatement. "No, I am certainly not." Then she sobered. "The truth is, I don't know where I'm going, except away from Mycenae."

"Where is your family? Your home?"

"My family is dead, and my home was destroyed," she said heavily.

Charis simply nodded. "The war?"

"Yes."

"I'm so sorry. Will anyone come looking for you?"

Kassandra stared into the dark before answering. "There is no one left. No."

Charis put a consoling arm across Kassandra's shoulders and said, "Travel with us, at least until you know where you're going. We will eventually arrive in Elis, our home. Perhaps you will find a new home there as well."

Kassandra turned to her, hardly able to believe what Charis offered. "I could never repay such generosity." It was barely above a whisper.

"Nonsense. I'm sure you'll be able to make yourself useful." Kassandra met a steady gaze and a warm, sincere smile. She could barely speak her gratitude for the tightness in her throat. Charis squeezed her shoulders. "Everyone needs a little help now and then. For starters, let's find you some practical clothing."

Kassandra did find a way to contribute. There was no healer with them, but having been one of Apollo's priestesses, she had learned herb lore and basic healing arts. On the first day, she wrapped Galenos's ankle and made a poultice to help with the swelling. A tea she made with a bit of nightshade leaf eased the headaches Sophia often fell victim to.

She was wary of Phaidros and Linos at first, concerned they might recognize her, but they didn't seem to. Linos was a large man, the kind one expected to be boisterous; instead he was almost too quiet, and his eyes held an eternally haunted look. On the second night, when they gathered around a large, single fire, Sophus asked Linos and Phaidros about Troia's fall. It took a moment for Linos to answer.

"After ten years, they became men possessed," he said distantly. "Like maddened dogs. They killed without conscience. Old men, little children. What they did to the women," Linos choked at the horrors in his memory, horrors Kassandra saw all too vividly in her own. Phaidros put a hand on his friend's shoulder and took up the tale.

"Even in camp, we could hear the terrified screams. They sacked the temples—all of them." Charis gasped, and Sophia made the sign of Hermes. "We were with King Nestor, and he ordered his men back, said we would take no part in desecration. We loaded our ship and waited. We weren't alone. Two other generals also refused. We don't even know if they found Sparta's queen. When a thunderbolt struck in front of Athena's temple, we set sail. We were just ahead of the main fleet. The violent storms we saw behind us were constant. Half the ships were lost. We didn't stop praying the entire voyage. King Nestor said our piety spared us."

In Kassandra's opinion, the gods' punishment of the Achaeans for their sacrilege was too little, too late. Where were the gods when her people were being slaughtered? Surely, no one deserved such a fate. At this point, she wished simply for the gods, one and all, to leave her alone.

Later that night, Kassandra arranged the bed roll Charis had given her. She'd also received two sturdy chitons, a pair of heavy-soled sandals, and a good shawl in trade for the gown and travel cloak. Now, she lay with the stars spread across the sky above her, a beautiful river of light. When was the last time she'd noticed them? The soft sounds of the settling camp surrounded her. Drifting off to sleep, she marveled at her incredible turn of fortune.

The days passed in peace, although Kassandra was sore the first week, being unaccustomed to walking great distances. The main road was paved, but they often turned onto well-traveled dirt ones to trade in the smaller towns. Growing up in Troia, she was used to the harsh beauty of sand and stone. The cool, peaceful green of Greece was a welcome change. She had never seen so many trees! Kassandra felt her previous life fade. She was Eurayle now, who spent her time cataloging the herbs they stocked, determining how much to save and how much could be sold or traded. They stopped in towns for a few days at a time, and a week in Arkadia for Philon's dedication ceremony. She was even learning how to cook from Sophia and Charis.

A different life, simpler, yet more labored, but she embraced it. These were not the Achaeans that attacked her city or murdered her people. They were good, honest, and decent. They didn't judge her, and no one pried into her past.

A month since the orchard, they were encamped near the town of Tritea when an all too familiar headache woke her. Something dreadful was about to happen. She groaned and rolled over on the blanket in a futile attempt to ignore Apollo's so-called gift.

It came anyway: Starkly vivid, staccato images. Their caravan—a crack reverberates. "Area's always been safe, we can stay." Night—camp fire. A swarm of men—travelers? Or soldiers? A crow laughs—pools of blood.

Kassandra screamed.

"Euralye, wake up," Sophia was beside her, shaking her shoulders. "It's all right. It's just a nightmare."

Drowning in the images, gasping for breath, Kassandra managed to nod weakly. She couldn't tell Sophia what she'd seen or how it was far more than a night terror.

"That's it; breathe dear. Don't worry; the sun's bright and the morning clear. Some honeyed bread will chase your nightmare away."

No it won't, she thought. *Nothing will.*

Throughout the day Kassandra found herself distracted, obsessively watching carts for any sign of stress. She snapped at the children and jumped like a frightened hare when Kosmas came to ask about the herb supplies.

About an hour before Kosmas's usual camp site, a dreadful cracking echoed off the hillside. The sound was the knell of doom to Kassandra as she watched the lead cart tip to the right, a wheel buckling under it. Everyone ran to catch and pick up the spilling supplies while Kosmas and Phaidros examined the underside.

"It's the axle," Phaidros said. "I can fix and reinforce it, but it'll take me a day to get a makeshift forge ready."

"Well, this section of road has always been safe. We can stay here a couple of days."

"No," Kassandra moaned, "oh, no." Rushing to the rear of the caravan, she faced the rugged landscape behind them. She could leave in the night, go somewhere, anywhere, and save herself. *And leave them to their fate?* She paced back and forth. No, she couldn't, she wouldn't. She'd changed her future; she could change theirs! But how? She didn't notice that Sophia had followed her.

"You've been agitated all day, Eurayle." Kassandra spun around in alarm. Sophia peered at her thoughtfully. "By Gaia, what are you about?"

Kassandra could only clench her jaw in anguish.

"You're not one to get upset over trifles, but clearly you think something's wrong. What is it?"

"I . . . I can't tell you. I'm sorry, but I just can't."

"Why not?"

"Because," Kassandra looked down, "you won't believe me."

Sophia shook her head. "Not good enough. I've seen a lot over the years; you'd be surprised what I might believe."

Kassandra moved her mouth more than once, saying nothing, then closed her eyes in frustration. She had to calm down and regain her wits. Panic could make her blurt out the prophecy. Sophia slowly cocked her head.

"If I didn't know better, I'd think you were a mad woman."

Kassandra wasn't sure whether to laugh or cry. "You wouldn't be the first."

Sophia took her by the arm and led her, unresisting, to sit on the edge of the last cart. "Eurayle, do you know what I see when I look at you?" She asked quietly, but Kassandra shook her head. "First, a woman who was not always named Eurayle. Second, I see a young woman's face with an old woman's eyes. You've seen much, and there's considerably more to you than you admit. You hide it well enough, but not from me. Does that help loosen the dilemma you're in?"

Kassandra sighed.

"I'm sorry, Sophia. I don't intend to be difficult, but it's hard to explain."

Sophia raised her eyebrows. "It will not get any easier with silence."

Kassandra gazed into the distance. If she was going to try to save them, this was her opening. Squaring her shoulders, she looked directly at Sophia.

"I sometimes see the future," she stated bluntly.

Sophia blinked. "The gift of prophecy? Are you certain?"

"Oh, yes. Confirmed by the High

Priestess when I was a child. They called it a gift, too, said I was blessed by Apollo." She paused. "I used to see it that way."

"Prophecy can also be a great burden," Sophia said gently.

"I didn't know the god I venerated would eventually want payment for his gift." The bitterness in her own voice surprised her, and she took a moment to calm down again.

"I was fourteen, my life dedicated to serve Apollo as a virgin priestess. When he came to me, exalting my beauty and demanding I take him to my bed, I was confused. I thought this can't be, surely it's a test. So I refused his advances. To my shock, instead of praising me for passing his test, he became angry and cursed me. He decreed I would still have his gift of prophecy, but no one would ever believe me again."

"And you have had a vision involving the caravan." It was not a question. "But if you tell me what you saw— "

"The curse will compel you to think I am mad," Kassandra interrupted, "or worse, and ignore my warning. Disaster inevitably follows."

Sophia was contemplative, then slowly nodded. "Quite a dilemma." After a few minutes of silence, she stood up. "Come," she said, holding her hand out to Kassandra, "we will think of something."

Kassandra and Sophia came walking back toward the central fire. A man in well-worn travel garb was talking to Kosmas, who was laughing at something the man said. Clearly Kosmas was inviting him to stay for the evening. As the stranger turned his sallow, hawkish face into the light of the setting sun, the sound of his laugh was the caw of a crow. Kassandra stopped dead, Sophia stumbling into her.

Sophia grabbed her arm and pulled her behind the carts. Kassandra bit her knuckles in a renewed effort to resist the vision yearning to be told.

"Look at me!" Sophia snapped Kassandra's attention to her. "Think! I will not ask what you've seen, but you have seen it. Think. What can we do?"

For a long moment, all she could manage was to breathe, then Sophia's question filtered through the pounding of her heart. What could they do? It was just one man; where were the rest of them?

This wasn't the vision coming true yet. *Wait; yes it is. I saw traveler's garb and armor. It's a disguise. He's a spy!* Her father had used such men to gather information on rivals. If she could expose him, they would be warned without her telling the vision. But how could she fool such a man into betraying his purpose?

She looked at Sophia, epiphany and determination reining in her panic. Sophia smiled. "That's better. How can I help?"

"I'll need a carafe of the sweetest wine, just enough for one cup." Sophia nodded, and Kassandra headed for her herb chest.

It took an enormous force of will to school her features to pleasantness as she approached the spy who called himself Iorgus. They had long since finished another of Charis's fine meals, and the children were all settled in their beds. The men were talking axles, politics, and the upcoming games in Leontion.

"Iorgus, would you care for more wine?" Kassandra asked, catching his attention, which raked over her with barely suppressed lust.

"From a beauty like you, most certainly. Thank you."

She poured and smiled at him as he drank deeply.

"I'd like some more too, please." Kosmas said.

"I'm sorry, it's empty." She left, making a pretense of refilling the carafe with another cupful, while waiting for her concoction to take effect. By the time she returned, their guest was wavering like he'd had far more than two cups of wine. His face was slack and his eyes glassy, like his mind was far away.

She moved behind him, quietly asking, "Why are you here, Iorgus?" The man laughed and looked around conspiratorially.

"Shhh," he said, speech slightly slurred. "I'm a spy. We's gonna put you fools down. Take it all."

Gasps from the women, the men bristled, but Kassandra held up a hand. "The herbs suppress his inhibitions and judgment," she said. "He will answer any questions you ask, but you should ask carefully and quietly. Anger or fear can make the effect wear off faster."

Kosmas was no fool. He nodded and took a calming breath, the others watching in anxious silence. "Most people would hand over their coins without a fight. Why risk battle?"

"Tired o' pittances. And we's strong," the bandit said proudly. "Aniketos's got big plans, even got a horse! Can sell loot. Sell women an' brats. Get rich." Tessa began softly weeping, Georgios hugging her protectively.

"How strong are you?"

The man grinned. "Eleven. A few o' us got real armor and swords. Got 'em from Agememy-non's tin heads."

There were soft grunts of alarm, a growl from Linos, "damn" from Phaidros. Kosmas held up his hand emphatically.

"When will you attack?"

"Tomorrow. Moonrise."

"From the north?"

"Nah, east. Over the hill. So's you don't see us comin'." He giggled and tried to drink from his drained cup, then peered in mournfully. "Can I have more?"

"We should kill him now," Phaidros whispered, but Linos disagreed.

"If we do, his companions will know we're on guard. Better to let him go."

"But he'll tell them he's talked," warned Kosmas.

"Not if he can't remember," Kassandra said.

The others watched warily as she dropped crushed herbs into the carafe, swirling it before refilling Iorgus's cup. He swallowed it in one gulp. Kassandra sat in front of him and waited for signs of the mixture's effects.

"Look at my eyes, Iorgus," she said in a singsong voice. "Do you like my eyes?"

He smiled crookedly. "Pretty eyes."

"Keep watching my eyes."

She began a slow, rhythmic back and forth swaying, his eyes tracking hers. His gaze became vacant.

"Listen to my voice. Only my voice. You're going to close your eyes now; you're very tired."

"Tired," he echoed.

"You've had a wonderful time here,

with good food and wine. In the morning, you will thank Kosmas for his hospitality and report back to your friends everything was as expected. You will remember nothing else. Do you understand?"

"Unnerstand," he repeated dully.

"Sleep now."

He slid down beside the fire. In a moment he was snoring.

When she rose, Kassandra put a finger to her lips and motioned that they should move away. She followed them to the last cart.

Kosmas and Charis gave her an appraising look tinged with suspicion. Some of the others seemed apprehensive and unsure of what to think.

Kosmas intoned, "There is much we do not know about you, Eurayle."

She cast her eyes down, fearful she might still voice the prophecy and doom them all. Sophia came to her rescue.

"Trust me when I tell you not to ask, my son. She has my faith. What's important is we learned we are in peril and outnumbered."

Kosmas pondered a moment. "All right. So, how do we deal with this threat?"

"Deal?"Georgios retorted. "I think survive is a better word. Do we even have weapons? How are we to defend ourselves?"

"We should arrange the carts to give us protection," said Phaidros. "Find a way to shield the children."

"Well, I would be no good in a fight," Sophia said. "My body is stiff, and these old bones would break at a thought. Tessa here is too heavy with child to fight either. We can take the children into the western hills and hide there. We'll keep watch on the oxen, too." The young mother-to-be looked frightened but agreed. Sofia continued, "But you will need Charis and Eurayle here. They're strong enough, and you need numbers."

Kosmas turned to Charis, putting his hand on hers. "Reluctant as I am to put you in danger, my mother is right."

The fierceness in Charis' eyes would have quelled a king. "No one threatens my children," she growled and Kosmas nodded.

"Could we make traps or something?" Tessa asked with faint

hope.

"Excellent idea," said Phaidros. "But what?"

Kassandra looked over at the eastern hill the bandits planned to attack from. "The base of the hill on our side is in shadow. We could run a rope across to trip them."

"Yes," said Linos, "it will slow them down, and it might break some bones when they fall. Still, it will injure, not kill."

"I have a dozen iron spit tines I was delivering to Elis," said Sophus. "We could hide them upright in the grass."

"Might skewer a couple," nodded Phaidros, "maybe more maimed. Might not kill enough, but even maiming a few helps our odds."

"We could tip the tines with poison," Kassandra said, her heart pounding as all eyes turned to her.

"Poison?" Georgios sputtered.

"Yes. I can make a paste of concentrated nightshade to put on the tips. Even if it scratches them, the poison will get in."

Sophia cocked her head, bemused. "Isn't nightshade what you put in my tea?"

"It is. Tiny amounts of it ease pain; larger amounts impair coordination, cause confusion and false visions; but in pure form it's quite deadly."

Kosmas nodded. "These jackals are going to find we are not the easy targets they think we are."

They discussed strategy for some time. Phaidros said there were enough young trees to fashion several spears and Linos could teach basic spear combat and skirmish tactics. His reward for service included his heavy infantry gear: full armor, large shield, and xiphos, so at least he would be prepared.

Phaidros thought he could also make a javelin and atlatl, with Sophus to tinker the parts. If they could take out the leader, the rest might lose confidence. Discussing what could be efficiently done and learned in just one day, it sounded woefully inadequate; but even a small chance was better than none.

"I think we have as much of a plan as we can manage," Kosmas said.

"May the wings of Hermes be with us," Sophia added. Kassandra winced at the invocation, hoping no one noticed.

As they scattered toward their respective beds, Kosmas put his hand on Kassandra's arm. "I don't know how you knew, and my mother says I should not ask, but thank you. Your quick thinking may save us all."

It was a surreal day, dawning with the pretense of hospitality toward Iorgus. The awkward charade was mercifully brief. He solemnly thanked Kosmas just as instructed, then left. Linos, ostensibly collecting deadwood, watched him go. Afterward, he circled the camp to confirm that the spy had truly departed and there were no other lurkers.

From the moment they were certain of privacy, there was a flurry of activity while bewildered children looked on. Sophia forestalled their questions, simply telling them there was danger and they must do exactly as they were told. Obediently, they followed her and Tessa out of harm's way, herding the oxen with them.

The men unloaded the other supply carts, moving them into place along with the broken cart and turning them on their sides; then the three tented carts were moved in, forming a circular defense line where the five men could cover the single opening.

Charis and Sophus strung the rope after first coating it in mud to help conceal it as much as possible. It was attached to a tree on one side and the shard of broken axle driven deep into the ground on the other. Then they pounded each tine into the ground two paces in front of the trip rope.

Kassandra spent much of the day brewing her toxic paste then carefully applying it to the tine points. There was just enough left to coat two of their spears. In the afternoon, Linos gave them what fighting lessons he could. They stopped before dusk to make sure they were rested, fed, and in position. Then, they waited.

"Remember," Linos reminded the men as they got into position, "our goal is to survive long enough to convince them that we aren't worth the trouble.

Don't take unnecessary risks. Stab them if you get a good chance, but mainly stay in your places and keep them back. Whatever you do, don't get drawn away from our battle line. In the open, they'll overwhelm you. Avoid the swordsmen. I'll deal with them."

The full moon was peeking through the tree line when the band charged over the eastern rise.

Kassandra, like Charis, lay under a tent cart by the opening the bandits had to use, each armed with a poison-coated spear. She watched as the first two bandits fell victim to the trip rope and tines with surprised yelps and howls of pain. Two more were snagged less soundly, but they were slowed. It was hard to tell who successfully jumped or skirted around, although she thought at least one more got scratched. Kassandra wished the nightshade a quick journey.

The bandits' leader, Aniketos, riding in the back, paused at the unexpected events. Linos took the opportunity to hurl the javelin, striking him and toppling him off his horse. The battle was quickly becoming less one sided than expected.

Linos, in full gear, drew his xiphos and confidently engaged both Iorgus and the other armored bandit, blocking and parrying their swings. The second swordsman moved ponderously, clearly unaccustomed to the weight of his ill-fitting stolen armor. The rest of the line fended off leather-clad ruffians with their spears. On Linos's immediate left, Sophus doggedly fought his attacker; on his far left, Kosmas repeatedly tried to stab an able dodger. On Linos's immediate right, young Georgios was having trouble holding his position, but his attacker showed blood trickling down from a scratch on his leg. Georgios just had to hold on until the poison could do its work. At his far right, Phaidros's steady defense forced his foe to hang back cautiously.

Kosmos was near the cart Charis was under, Paidros near Kassandra's. Two of the bandits were circling obliquely to each side of the scrum, an attempt to double-team the two brothers. Kassandra carefully anticipated the rightward one's approach, slashing him behind the knee as he passed. The bandit squealed and sprawled on his side, his leg no longer holding his weight. He crawled desperately away, to her immense satisfaction.

A shout of, "Gaaah, get them off!" plus a high-pitched keening came from the base of the hill. Kassandra smiled grimly as the wailing became blubbering whimpers. The poison was doing its work.

Charis's swipe missed its mark, only managing to prick the left approaching bandit between his sandal straps. She tried to duck back but wasn't quick enough. The bandit scrambled after her with an irate roar. He yanked her out by one foot and started dragging her off. Pitched onto her back, she was trying to resist when her spear caught in the spokes of the wheel and was snagged out of her grip.

"Charis!" Kosmas made a desperate lunge to bypass his assailant, and Phaidros yelled, "No!"

Kosmas's dodger took advantage of his divided attention and body-slammed Kosmas, knocking him off balance, then clubbed him with the cheek of his hatchet, and Kosmas dropped.

Charis's shriek of panic and grief

sliced through the clamor, and something in Kassandra snapped. Abandoning her hiding place, she lapsed into her native Luwian with a blood-curdling scream of primal rage.

The world around her turned red and slowed to a crawl. Kosmas's attacker bent to finish him off, then straightened and twisted at the piercing sound. With berserk strength, Kassandra swept a vicious, high slash across his throat. He recoiled and dropped, spraying gouts of crimson.

Kassandra burst through the gap where Kosmas had been standing, brandishing her spear like an Amazon, screaming Luwian curses. Linos's command, "Eurayle, stop!" meaningless to her ears.

Kassandra leveled the spear, charging the bandit grappling with a frantically kicking Charis. He dropped Charis and tried to ready himself. Too late.

"Not again!" Kassandra shouted as the spear plunged into him. "Never again," she hissed in his face. He slumped to the ground, taking the embedded spear with him. A dagger flipped out of his slackened hand, and she snatched it up, spinning to take in the main battle, blood roaring in her ears.

Sophus's attacker disarmed and knocked him down, rendering the tinker defenseless. Kassandra flung the dagger with manic strength. It sailed true, embedding squarely in the man's back, and he folded.

"Eurayle?" Charis said incredulously, but it didn't seem relevant to Kassandra as she scanned the melee for the next object of her wrath. Instead, the pale moonlight revealed a lurid scene of carnage. An armored body spasmed, its head rolling away while Linos next disarmed and dispatched Iorgus. Phaidros's foe was impaled and sinking to the ground. The bandit on Georgios was swinging wildly, shouting at specters only he could see. The scholar managed to avoid the wide, staggering slashes to finish the brute off. With the last enemy dead, Kassandra stood shaking in the ghostly quiet as her bloodlust slowly subsided.

Charis ran to where Kosmas's lay sprawled. "Eurayle!" She called. "Please!

Help him!"

Kassandra didn't respond. Linos touched her shoulder, and she whirled, eyes wide and feral. He caught her by the arms and shook her gently but firmly, making her look at him.

"Eurayle! It's over. We're safe."

"Linos," she said as focus started coming back.

"Can you help Kosmas?"

She looked down at him. "Kosmas." She bent to examine his wound, then headed to the cart she kept her supplies in.

Kassandra rummaged in the chest, fumbling, her head spinning as she tried to concentrate through the fog of draining adrenaline. She needed bandages and yarrow for the bleeding. The pain would have to wait; head wounds could be complicated.

She'd taken two steps away from the cart when she heard the muffled clink of cloaked armor. A strong arm grabbed her by the throat, pinning her to the man's chest, choking her. His other arm came up to hold a sword across her chest.

"Well, if it isn't Princess Kassandra,

Agamemnon's royal whore!" The leader had survived the javelin.

She struggled, but his grip on her throat only tightened. Sophus and Georgios stood by Charis, while Phaidros and Linos came running.

"I'll snap her pretty neck," Aniketos warned. They skidded short. "Better. You've cost me plenty tonight. But this should more than cover it. King Agamemnon will pay handsomely for his favorite concubine's return."

The man continued taunting, demanding that Linos and Phaidros drop their weapons, retrieve his horse, and help him leave, but the words were distant to Kassandra. She'd stopped struggling and started thinking.

She felt blood soaking onto the back of her shoulder. Not hers—his. He was wounded, desperate, and blustering to hide the tremor she could feel in his weakened sword arm.

He pulled her sideways with him as Phaidros walked the horse over. All she needed was a bit of leverage. Yes, his horse would do nicely.

Kassandra savagely dug jagged nails into the wrist of his sword hand as she slammed her head back into his wounded shoulder. He gasped and spasmed, the grip on her neck loosening just enough for her to sink her teeth into his hand. She tasted blood as the bandit leader shrieked, involuntarily shoving her away and stumbling backward. The sword fell from his grip, and she grabbed it. End heavy, it took both hands for her to control it.

"Agamemnon is with Hades," she snarled, raising the sword like the queen's axe. "And you can join him!"

It slammed down, splitting his skull with a hideous crunch. She wrenched it free of the quivering corpse and raised it again, but Linos caught her wrists.

"Trust me, he's dead." He gently wrested the blade from her grip. "Go help Kosmas."

Hours later, Kosmas was bandaged and resting, doted on by a much relieved Charis. The bandit bodies were dragged to the other side of the hill they'd attacked from, leaving them for the scavengers. They carefully gathered up all the spikes, then Phaidros whistled the all clear signal to Sophia. Kassandra sat staring into the fire as Phaidros and Linos joined her.

"What he called you," Linos said quietly, "is there something we should know?"

Kassandra looked up at him. Linos's eyes still held the echo of memories he would rather not have—of all of them, he most understood what she wished to forget.

"Princess Kassandra died in Mycenae, executed by Queen Clytemnestra. That is the official record. I am simply Eurayle, no more and no less."

"I do not think you will ever be simple," Phaidros rumbled, and Linos grunted in amusement.

"Here come Sophia and the children," Phaidros said, changing the subject. There was no need to bring it up again.

ON THIN ICE
by
Cat Greenberg

If you've ever wondered where storytellers get their ideas, here's one answer. When I lived in Maryland, there was a swamp across from the entrance to our subdivision. During particularly bad winters, it was frozen over, the trees covered in ice, and seemed always shrouded in a misty fog. It was eerie, foreboding, and enchanting all at the same time, and there was the seed of a story, imagining an ice swamp in the middle of a desert.

Ara sped at full gallop straight for The Shining Death. As the miles of desert sand passed under her and the deadly, glittering tower-like trees grew larger, the foundation of the plan she'd hastily formed a few hours earlier began to crumble.

No one in their right mind went *toward* Gelidad-Bahir. Then again, Ara was certain she was as far from right minded as possible. She glanced back at the plume of dust in the distance behind her.

Ara'd been sent to fetch a girl who'd caught the eye of Prince Malik. It was a duty she was far too familiar with, and so she'd knocked on the door of Ashraf and asked for his daughter Linia. But when Linia came to the door beside her father, something in Ara broke. *This* was who Prince Malik wanted in his bed as a distraction? A child as yet not even to her twelfth year?

"I can't do it," she'd stammered. "I won't do it. Leave," she told Ashraf. "By the north gate. There's a caravan leaving at sunset; you can buy your way onto it. If you wish to save your child, leave."

She'd given them what coinage she had and returned to the palace, thinking fast. She wouldn't live past sunset for refusing a direct order from Her Majesty's Firstborn. Best make it worth it. After setting some crude but carefully placed traps and tangles, she unleashed a decade of frustration and grievance on her despised captain, leaving Ferin and her favorites senseless on the floor. Then, seeing Malik in the courtyard, she shouted precisely what she thought of the arrogant, useless excuse of a First Born Prince as she'd ridden past him.

Pulling to a stop, Ara slid off her trembling horse, apologizing for having ridden him so hard. She looked up at the immense ice-covered tree-towers and tried to peer into the white haze of frozen bog.

She'd heard the stories all her life. Those who tried to cross through Gelidad-Bahir's twenty-mile width were never seen again. It was said to be a cursed place, full of demons. Never-melting ice in the heart of a burning desert. Even the Visaris' most hardened soldiers feared to cross its icy threshold and would not follow her there. At least, that was her plan. Facing it, she found herself wondering if she was going to be able to cross into it herself.

She held up her hand. Standing in the scorching sun made the cool air emanating from the edge inviting. She'd never seen ice before. It mesmerized, sparkling in the afternoon sun. She'd only half believed the stories of Aldebar and the wizards who once ruled the world. Their existence seemed more fable than history, until now. How could anything but magic have created this? And did it mean the other stories were also true? That this harsh land of sand and stone was once green and fertile before those same wizards went to war, giving rise to places like Jaylis and breeding the likes of the Visaris.

The sound of thundering hooves reached her, and she looked from the rapidly approaching riders to the ice and back again.

If she went in, unknown dangers awaited.

If she didn't, she faced danger she knew in great detail, having spent her first years of guard service in the Visaris' torture rooms. She still sometimes heard the screams of the prisoners in her dreams.

Ara slung her large waterskin over her head, pulled the saddle off, grabbed the blanket underneath, and then patted her horse farewell. She could tell by the whites of his eyes that she would never convince him to enter the swamp. Just as the riders were pulling up, she entered The Shining Death.

I don't have to go far, she thought.

If they believed her lost, they'd give up and go back to Jaylis, where she'd be just another story told to frighten children into obedience. Then, she could make a life for herself elsewhere. Perhaps the mistake others made was trying to cross Gelidad-Bahir. If she stayed just inside the edge, she wouldn't get lost.

She was unprepared for how slippery the ice was, and the frozen grass crunched and shifted under her feet. She reached for a vine for balance, but it shattered in her hand, and her feet came out from under her. Gnarled, frozen tree roots as hard as rocks slammed into her hip. She clenched her jaw on an invective, knowing how close the guards were, and slid hand over hand around until she was behind the tree.

"Ara!" shouted Captain Ferin, and Ara silently chastised herself for not having gutted the woman. "Ara!"

Puzzled by the muffled and distant

sound of Ferin's voice, Ara peered around the trunk. The party wavered like heat on the sand; she rubbed her eyes, but her vision didn't clear. Why did they look so blurry? She'd gone, at most, ten paces into the trees.

"Go away, Ferin," she shouted from behind the tree. "Unless you want to come in and get me!"

"Ara! Answer me!"

"I already did, you . . ." she scowled and carefully pulled herself up for a better view. Ferin was looking all around, trying to see into the swamp, but she didn't know which direction to look. Ara picked her way around the frozen trunk to stand in what should have been Ferin's full view. She looked right at Ara but made no indication that she saw her.

"Ferin!" she shouted. "You're a three-eyed, six-legged sand rat!"

No reaction. Ara could see and hear Ferin, yet she apparently couldn't see or hear Ara, even standing this close.

This could be fun, she thought.

Ara watched in fascination as the troop of guards paced along the edge. Someone in the back dismounted and stalked forward. Ara gasped as the green and gold form of the Eldest approached the edge. Then, she laughed.

"Hah! Made you leave your comfortable palace and chase me across the desert, I did! If I die tomorrow, it was worth it just for that, you worthless piece of scarp dung!" She goaded in the certainty he couldn't hear her.

Ferin dropped to one knee before the Eldest.

"Eminence, she has entered Gelidad-Bahir. She is surely lost."

Malik glared down at his captain, then kicked Farin in the face, sending her sprawling. When Ferin recovered her place, Malik smiled maliciously.

"She did not choose to enter, Captain Ferin. I personally threw her in after stripping her of her rank and her uniform. Is that understood?"

Only the briefest confusion crossed Ferin's bloodied face before she said, "Yes, Eminence."

"Liar!" Ara shouted. There was no reaction. "Someday, someone is going to shove that pride of yours right down your throat, Malik! I just wish I could be there to see it." She grunted. "I wish I could be there to *do* it."

They gathered themselves to go. Ara unfolded the horse blanket, settled it around and under her as best she could, and sat against the tree. She would wait until she was certain they were out of sight of the threshold, then she'd creep out, follow the perimeter, and head south or east. She could sleep during the day, then walk during the cool of night. Sila'an was twice the distance to the east that Jaylis was to the north, but if she rationed her water, she had a fair chance.

She closed her eyes to rest.

Cold.

It was the first sensation to reach her consciousness as she awoke—cold so deep it touched her bones.

For a moment she was confused. She'd been chilled before, in the desert air at night, but this kind of cold was a new sensation. She opened her eyes, then straightened abruptly. Pain lightninged through her body, and she cried out. No part of her was spared the stiffening cold.

The ice swamp.

She was inside Gelidad-Bahir.

Events restored themselves to her memory, and she stood, pulling the blanket closer around her. *Time to get out of here.*

She took a step in the direction she thought was the threshold and stopped, perplexed. Her brow creased. This looked wrong. No, this couldn't be the way; it showed only more trees and swamp.

She turned the other way and stopped again, met by an identical view. She swallowed, dread clawing at her empty stomach as she slowly turned a full circle.

Every direction looked exactly the same!

This was impossible. She'd only come into the trees a few paces, ten at most. She ought to be able to see the desert; it was broad daylight! Wasn't it?

It wasn't dark; it wasn't exactly light either.

She held out her hand. No shadow fell below it. The light was a dull white glow filling the spaces between the brighter white of the frozen trees and brush.

Ara took a deep breath, determined to quell her growing panic. She hugged the horse blanket closer as her breath plumed out.

"Okay," she said, talking out loud to calm her shaking insides. "What are my choices? If I stay here, at the least, I'll starve. Should have grabbed food on the way out." She paced a small path in front of the tree. "From the way I feel, I can assume too much cold can kill the same as too much heat. So, sitting here isn't much of an option. I never liked sitting around anyway, but which way do I go?"

Did it matter? All the views were the same. She loosened the thick braid of black hair crowning her head and coiled it about her neck for warmth. She tucked the horse blanket around her shoulders, securing it in her belt, then started off, choosing a direction at random.

Ara's foot slipped for what felt like the hundredth time. The bog ice cracked, and her foot slid into slush beneath. Cold pain pierced her foot as her boot filled with ice water. A guttural scream erupted as she challenged the swamp as a whole.

"I thought there were supposed to be demons in here!" She pulled herself back up and leaned against a tree, panting. "So where are you?" The shout died away to an angry mutter. "I could use a good fight right now."

What am I doing here? She asked herself yet again. *Saving some sprig of a girl I don't even know? And what if he's caught them anyway? Stupid plan, could've been for nothing for all I know.*

Ara's teeth chattered, and she bit her lip to stop it. In the heat of the desert sun, she'd tried to imagine what ice might feel like; now she regretted ever wondering. She leaned her head back to rest against the tree, her eyes slowly closing. She was so cold, so tired.

"foreversleep"

Her eyes flew open, her sword flashing out of its sheath to threaten the cold, empty air.

"Who said that?" she demanded. Stillness answered her. Had she imagined it?

"eyescloseforeversleep"

A faint, lilting whisper, like the wind

was talking; only there wasn't the slightest breeze. Was it enticing her to sleep? Or warning against it?

"Show yourself!"

"whoareyou"

It sang the question, all the words running together on a sigh of sound that filled the air despite its quietness.

"I am Ara of the Visaris' Royal Guard in Jaylis. Who are you?" She pointed the sword at the air in general.

"whoareyou"

Seeing no threat, Ara slammed the sword home in its sheath. "This is pointless," she said and trudged on. With each step, a vicious stabbing lanced through her wet foot and up her leg. Ice formed on the leather of her boot. She slipped again and cursed, catching herself painfully on a small tree.

"whoareyou"

"My luck," she grumbled, flexing stiff and numbing fingers. "Instead of a demon with substance I get a disembodied spirit obsessed with my identity."

"whoareyou"

"A half-frozen idiot, that's who! One

who should have stayed where it's warm." She pulled her fingers into the palms of her gloves to warm them. It hardly helped and left her unable to hold on to the branches for balance. She sighed and extended the fingers again, grabbing onto whatever she could as she walked.

"whoareyou"

"Will you stop asking me that? I already told you!"

"whoareyou"

Ara whirled around angrily and lost her footing. The back of her head hit the knotted trunk of a frozen tree and her vision tunneled.

"Leave me alone!" she raged.

She sank the rest of the way down, her head spinning miserably.

"whoareyou"

"I told you, Ara of the Visaris' Royal Guard. Or was. Threw that away, didn't I?" At least talking was helping to clear her aching head. "What do you want, my life story?" She asked sarcastically as she pulled herself upright. "So I guess I'm back to being just a gutter-rat orphan. Had a mother; her name was Danil. She was a barmaid for an innkeeper named Ashir. Never met the man who sired me. All I know is he was a rich caravan owner who demanded more than a barmaid should ever have to give." Ara started walking again, pulling herself hand over hand from tree to tree.

"Only Ashir didn't see it that way." Ara's eyes smoldered with hate at the memory of her mother's employer. "You ever been to Jaylis, Spirit? Wonderful place, Jaylis. They say you can buy anything in the market there. In fact, a piece of gold can even buy a man's conscience. And Ashir was offered five! All he had to do was deliver my mother to the merchant's room and walk away. He left an untried girl of fifteen to be passed around all night by four drunk men. She'd never been with a man before; that's why they wanted her. And she never laid with a man again. They broke her of ever wanting to. No lovers, no husband. I was twelve when she died." Ara paused, climbing over a mound of frozen plants she didn't recognize. "Been on my own since."

Ara stopped to take a drink, only to discover the water skin was a solid block of ice.

"Damn," she muttered. "At least it should melt once I get out of here."

"whoareyou"

"Gutter rat, sand flea, dung cousin, bastard. Take your pick. I've been called them all. You know what the biggest curse to a girl is, Spirit? Being pretty. Exotic, they called me, 'cause of the black hair and black eyes. Gifts from the seed that sired me. But I remembered what my mother taught me. No man will ever have me like that, and two are dead for trying."

She made it over the mound but slipped on the other side. Sharp ice caught on the blanket, ripping it. She clutched it tighter around her. She had to keep moving. If she stopped, she might not be able to start again.

"whoareyou"

"Crazy spirits. You're supposed to be ten feet tall with four heads, blood-dripping fangs, fire for eyes and claws sharp enough to rip souls. Did you know that, Spirit? I'm disappointed. You just don't sound like all the stories I was raised on."

"whoareyou"

"An orphan, that's who." This was getting annoying, but she kept answering. It was better than silence. "A fighter. And a killer. In Jaylis, you kill or you die. Or worse. Only law a child of the streets knows. At twenty, I sheathed my sword in Ashir's fat belly for what he let them do to my mother. And I made sure he knew exactly who I was, too. Next day, I killed the Visaris' champion and won a place in her Legion. Fought my way up to Royal Guard." Another hand-held branch broke, and her shoulder hit painfully against the trunk.

"Then, I stupidly entered this bloody cold swamp of yours!"

She started to climb another mound. It was taller, and she pulled out her sword, driving it into the ice-brush to help pull herself along.

"I threw it all away, Spirit. Everything I was, everything I'd known, all because I couldn't send a child to suffer what my mother had."

Her fingers weren't working right, and they felt bigger than they should. It was hard to tell if the foot that had plunged into the slush was supporting her. Were parts of her able to die while the rest struggled on? She was so tired. Was it night yet? The light never changed here. How long had she been walking? She'd just told a disembodied spirit the story of her life, a life that seemed an eternity gone. She couldn't remember what warmth felt like anymore. The scorching desert sun seemed as insubstantial as a half-remembered dream. The only thing real was the bone-searing cold.

Each step became slower than the last as she pulled herself farther. Her wet foot came out from under her, and she lost her grip on the hilt and plunged head-first back down the slope and landed in a tangle of icy brush. Ara tried to push herself up, but her strength was spent. Her breath came in painful gasps, and her perception dulled. If parts of her were already dead, then perhaps it wouldn't hurt much for the rest to follow.

"whoareyou"

The spirit again, asking a question she thought she'd answered already. But had she? She'd told everything she had once been, but what was she now? Her name was all she had left of her miserable life.

Finally, she said, "I'm Ara. Just Ara."

The swamp glowed around her, the dull white turning dazzling before darkness engulfed her.

Ara became conscious of grass beneath her cheek and smiled at the wonderful dream. It smelled so sweet! She took a deep breath, savoring the scent. She flexed bare fingers in the soft, thick blades and opened her eyes. Blinked.

It *was* grass. *Real* grass. This wasn't a dream.

She pushed herself up sharply as the memory of ice surfaced. She'd been in Gelidad-Bahir. Was she dead?

She stood up slowly. She was on a hilltop. As far as she could see, the green grass spread out below her. She stared wide-eyed and open-mouthed at the sight of it. In the distance, she saw the expansive sparkle of . . . water! Could that be a lake? She'd heard tales of their existence long ago but had never seen one. In Jaylis, where men were known to kill for just a barrel of water, the idea of a huge expanse filled with it was almost beyond imagining.

"Good morning," came a musical voice from behind. She whirled, instinctively reaching for her sword. Of course, it wasn't there. It was still in the ice.

"Who are you?" Ara asked and remembered the spirit voice. Her eyebrows knitted together, then went up in surprise as she realized the sound of the greeting was the same. "You don't look like a four-headed, fanged demon."

The musical laughter enchanted her. Ara wasn't sure if she was addressing a woman or a man. Long hair of palest gold framed a face with the smooth skin of youth, but colorless eyes pierced Ara to the core, and in them she saw the kind of wisdom only immense age could bestow.

"I am the Guardian of the Gateway."

"What Gateway?"

"The one that cured you and transported you to this world." A delicate, long-fingered hand indicated the improbably green valley.

"I remember being cold." A still skeptical Ara folded her arms. "I don't remember opening any gates."

"It opens when at last you become simply yourself, free of all whom you have previously been. For only when you let go of your past are you ready to begin life anew."

Ara shook her head. "I was in Gelidad-Bahir. And I'm pretty sure I was dying. Is this the afterlife?"

The Guardian smiled, head cocked. "In a manner of speaking, I suppose it is. But, no, you did not die. I am the last Aldebarian wizard . . . "

Ara interrupted. "The ones in the stories? Who ruined the world, then left?"

Ara saw shame in those ancient eyes, and the pain of grief that will never heal. "Yes," the wizard admitted, "A fool's war. The tragedy yours, the blame ours."

"Do you have any idea what's grown out of the ashes? So, I guess you came here and lived comfortably while the Visaris took hold of what little you left!" Ara paced, venting anger, then whirled. "Why didn't you come back and fix it?"

"We tried, those who survived. Sadly, destruction is much easier than creation. We could not undo the damage. But the ice could be made a portal, saving the few desperate enough to brave what you have named Gelidad-Bahir. And who would more deserve the escape of a new life?"

"The stories," Ara said, "of no one ever returning—they all came here?"

"Yes. It is a one-way gate; there is no going back. Although so far, no one has asked to return. We can never make up for our crimes; we can only offer those like you a new life of freedom and peace." With that, the wizard faded to mist and was gone.

Ara stared at the spot where the wizard had been, agape more at what she'd heard than seen. In Jaylis, the powerful never apologized for anything. And this place? It was impossible, but she knew it was real. No dream or sweet illusion conjured by her dying mind would have included a wizard offering penance.

Ara had lived for the past until she'd avenged her mother. After that, she'd lived in the here and now, for having a future was never assured in bitter Jaylis. Here and now, she stood in a world green and beautiful. She'd seen ice for

the first time; now it was time to see her
first lake.

REPUTATIONS
by
Cat Greenberg

This story actually began as a song, "Salvaging Andromeda's Ghost." *When Captain Quinn introduced herself to me, the song became the story outline.*
An old-fashioned pirate ghost story. With space ships.

Captain Zyra Quinn sighed as she looked over the far too short catalog of the Brigato's recent salvage. They'd found a freighter that had lost power and ran afoul of a nasty asteroid field. The damage hadn't left much worth salvaging. They needed a better haul before going back to Orion Yard or she wouldn't be able to make her insurance, dock fees, and the all-important loan payment, let alone buy fuel for another run. And that was on top of not being able to pay her crew, who deserved better. The last time they were this strapped, they'd had to take a job ferrying prisoners to the penal colony on Io. Two years later there were still areas of the hold that reeked of urine. She hated to wish misfortune on others, but they needed to find another wreck.

"Captain," her pilot, Alek Rigatos, called over the com, "we got a dead one."

There's timing for you, Zyra thought as she came onto the bridge from her office.

"Transponder?" she asked.

"Receiving." He paused, his brow furrowed, and he punched buttons before looking up in astonishment. "That's the Andromeda's Ghost!"

"What would a yacht like her be doing out here? Check your readings." Alek was a fine pilot at twenty-four but still a bit green in the experience department and too eager to accept a first reading. She'd been trying to drill that into him lately, so she wasn't surprised when his voice held an edge of annoyance.

"I did check them. Twice."

Zyra leaned over his chair. The

listing ship was still too far away for eyes, visible only to the sensitive long-range sensors. The transponder registered unmistakably on Alek's board: Andromeda's Ghost, registry DSMC1437, Deimos Station, Mars Colony.

"What in Sol's name would the Rybar daughters be doing out here?"

"The Ghost is the fanciest hot rod in the system," Alek sighed in appreciation of the kind of ship he would likely never be wealthy enough to pilot. "Their father even hired an all-female crew for it. He said it was to protect the honor of his blood."

Zyra stood up and grunted in disgust. "Bunch of socialites with more money than sense. The air-headed fools had no business taking a joy ride out here. Look what it got them. How long until we know if they survived?"

"Thirty minutes, give or take."

"Keep me posted. I'm getting lunch."

Zyra ran her hand lovingly along the rough wall of the corridor as she walked to the galley. Let Alek envy yachts like the one floating dead out there; she didn't. Her *Brigato* had it where it counted. She couldn't offer her crew the highest wages, but she tried to give benefits other ships neglected. Crew quarters and galley were better appointed and more comfortable than most, shifts were reasonable, and leave was given whenever possible. The *Brigato's* engines might not be fancy, but they responded to Kagami Umari's ministrations like a lover. True, the hull hadn't seen fresh paint in a decade and was patched in no few places, but being pretty often attracts the wrong kind of attention—just ask any woman who's ever walked into a bar.

Zyra smelled the galley long before she walked through the door. It didn't matter how lean things got, Reneé Doylan made every meal taste like they were endlessly rich. She and Zyra went way back together, even before Zyra married Severin.

"Dinner smells good," she said.

"Thanks," Reneé called from the prep room. "Bet you need some lunch."

"Whatever's easy," Zyra called.

Reneé came in with a sandwich and stopped a moment before setting it on the counter in front of her friend. "You're worried."

"Yeah. I just looked at the list from the last salvage. Not much, and not enough." She took a bite of the sandwich. "But we just picked up a ship that seems dead."

"Good prospect?"

"Still too far out, but we'll see. Looks like a Mars yacht."

"A yacht? Out here?"

"Yeah, makes no sense, but when do 'Ristos ever make sense?" The Mars Colony aristocracy had never impressed Zyra as having much in the brain cell department, and this proved it. "Especially those two—if the readings are true, it's the Ghost."

"The Rybar sisters? Out here? Probably doing another stupid look-how-rich-we-are vid."

"Must be nice to have nothing more to worry about than star gowns, parties, and how many men are vying for your attention," Zyra said in disgust.

She was just finishing her coffee when Alek called down.

"Cap'n, you'd better see this."

The two women looked at each other.

Alek sounded spooked. Zyra tossed her plate in the cleaner and punched the com. "On my way."

The lift stopped, and Zyra stepped onto an eerily silent bridge. Marlis and Jeorg Ziegler had joined Alek. Marlis was her engineering assessor. She knew the current trade value of the drive systems, consoles, navigation computers—anything that was a part of the mechanical working of the ship. Her younger brother knew the value of the more esoteric bits: fixtures, furniture, personal property, even the occasional embarrassing holo. He also had all the right connections for finding appropriate buyers.

"What we got?" Zyra asked taking her chair.

"Pirate hit," Alek answered. "And look at the pattern. No hull breeches, surgical strikes to the engines, left environmental untouched."

Zyra gave a grim sigh. Everyone on the bridge knew this pattern of attack meant only one thing.

"Slavers. Any sign of life?" She knew the answer but asked anyway, slim as the hope was.

"Nothing registers," Alek answered.

"An all-woman crew on a weaponless yacht with socialite passengers? Quite a haul for a slaver. They'd have headed straight for the Rim with that lot."

"Slavers don't strip the ship, at least not excessively," said Jeorg, "could be a good haul for us."

"If they left the logs, maybe we can get a reading on who did it," added Marlis. "Think old man Rybar would pay well for a lead he can follow? Might allow him to send hired guns to retrieve his kin."

Zyra spun around to glare at Marlis.

"If found, the 'old man' will not be charged for such information," Zyra said in a tone brokering no argument.

"Yes, ma'am," Marlis said, looking chagrined. They were all on edge; everyone knew the financial situation, but there were some things that just should not have a price.

"I hate slavers," Zyra muttered as she turned back to the screen. There was silence as composure was regained, then she was all business. "Gear up; we've got work to do. Thirty minutes to dock. And call Severin; always good to have the medic along, just in case. You said life support's up?"

Alek pulled up the information. "Atmosphere, gravity—all check normal—temperature's twenty-two C."

"Good, work's always easier without full suits. Alek, you and Kag keep the engines hot and your eyes open, I don't want any unpleasant surprises. Let's go."

The air locks mated and cycled. Zyra, Marlis, Jeorg and Severin stepped through their own, waited for it to close, then stepped into the *Andromeda's*. The outer hatch closed, and the inner one opened. As they stepped into the dark ship, all four gasped.

"Alek!" Zyra yelled into the com. "You said environmental was on line. It's colder than vacuum in here!"

"Impossible," Alek responded, "All the readings say normal."

"I'll check it," said Severin, rubbing his arms against the cold. Before he made it to the glowing wall console, the cold was gone.

"What just happened?" Marlis asked.

"Cap'n?" Asked Alek.

Zyra and her crew exchanged looks, "Just a glitch, Alek, it's fine now." Then to Severin, "Get the lights up."

Severin punched a series of buttons, and the lights came on, showing an entrance bay with pale green walls.

"That's better."

"No sign of a firefight in here. I wonder if they mounted any defense?" Marlis had no patience for women who played at being helpless as she held numerous championship belts for a variety of fighting styles.

"If they had no weapons, what could they do?" Asked Jeorg, defending the missing crew.

"Anything can be a weapon in the right hands," she told him.

"Not everyone is you, sis."

"Gonna be a pretty empty ship," Severin changed the subject and headed for a door opposite the air lock.

The door slid open on a corridor with walls of variegating shades of green and plush blue, anti-static carpet.

"This will fetch a nice price if we can get it up in one piece," said Jeorg appreciatively. "Or I could just use it in my quarters."

"Bills first," Zyra reminded him. She checked her handheld and motioned left. "Bridge is this way; we'll start there. Slavers take some personal stuff but tend to leave equipment. Boat like this'll have state of the art. You got the shopping list from Kag?" Before anything was cataloged for sale, her engineer always got first dibs on equipment that could augment the *Brigato*.

"Yeah, I got it," answered Marlis.

They headed down the corridor. As they turned a corner, there were three pirate bodies in the threshold of the door. All were wearing the same rough uniform, nothing the fashionable Rybar sisters would have used, and all were men. Severin rolled each over in turn, checking for signs of life.

"They're dead," he confirmed.

"Guess the ladies put up a fight after all," said Jeorg, but Marlis only grunted.

"Good for them," Zyra said, stepping carefully past the bodies.

At the lift there were four more dead After checking them, Severin pulled Zyra aside.

"I don't like this, Zyra. There's not a mark on them, same as the others. The bio scanner is reading coronary."

Zyra scowled. The three previous bodies were young men, easily under thirty. These were two men and two women, but none looked more than forty.

"Chemical?" Zyra asked. "You think there's a danger? Are we exposed?"

"Possibly, but I'm not picking anything up."

"A new poison? One the handheld doesn't recognize?"

"Could be; a new one pops up every few years. Caution would be advised."

"Hazmat masks, people," Zyra ordered. "There could be chemicals about. These weren't felled by a gun."

"More to our socialites than meets the eye," came grudging admiration from Marlis.

"Apparently," said Zyra.

They pulled the bodies away from the lift and got in. The doors opened on the bridge, and another blast of icy air hit them, gone as quickly as it came but this time accompanied by the smell of blood.

"This is the freakiest environmental glitch," Zyra said, checking the handheld as Jeorg stepped through the door first.

A gargled sound escaped him as he flung himself over the bridge railing, violently emptying his stomach, the mask he'd been wearing flung aside. Marlis gasped then focused her gaze on the floor while she tried to help her brother.

"By all that's holy," Zyra whispered, barely keeping her own lunch down.

"I don't think holy has anything to do with it," Severin said flatly.

There were five naked men trussed upside down, secured to open beams where the fancy ceiling tiles had been deliberately removed. All had clearly been tortured, and all of them had been castrated by something less than sharp. Blood pooled on the bridge floor from their wounds and slit throats.

"Find the logs," Zyra managed, trying to keep her mind on business. "Marlis!"

Marlis moved mechanically toward the console, keeping her eyes down to avoid the hanging bodies as she punched buttons.

"It's encrypted, Captain. It'll take some work."

"Download it; you can do it on *Brigato*."

A screech like metal being ripped with giant hands echoed through the bridge as Marlis worked to collect the data. The sound twisted, reverberating through bone and nerve alike, turning into a chorus of screaming voices torn from dying human throats. As the sound diminished, five men materialized in front of Zyra, who, along with the rest of her boarding party, defensively drew their sidearms. Then Zyra realized not only did the men simply stand there, but she could see the wall through them. She looked up to the bodies hanging from the beams and back to the translucent men and recognized every face as the same.

"I am Captain Bradford Sully of the slaver ship *Ravenger*," said the one in front. In life he must have been an intimidating figure, tall and well muscled. Even now he looked to be a man used to imposing his will on others. His voice was gravelly and rough with an unnatural echo that grated on raw nerves.

"My crew was feared throughout the Rim. The mere mention of the name *Ravenger* struck terror into the hearts of our foes. The number of women I've sold in the slave markets of Rimmark cannot be counted. We boarded this ship for the same reason, but it was a trap. We were ambushed in the corridors and here on the bridge by their witch. You can see how we died, our manhood taken as trophies while we yet lived, and our souls cursed as life drained from us. Our penance is to serve as a warning to those who find us of the rewards of our deeds."

With that, the men began to fade, leaving the bridge empty except for the bodies and themselves.

"Stupid holo prank," Zyra muttered.

"Captain," came a hoarse whisper from Jeorg, and she turned to him. He had recovered from his retching and was at one of the consoles, his face pale as a full moon. "This bridge has no holo emitters."

It took several long heartbeats for the import of this small fact to register in

Zyra's brain. Keeping a very tight leash on her reaction so as not to show how desperately she wanted to race for the airlock, she asked levelly, "Marlis, do you have the logs?"

"Yes, Cap'n," she answered, her voice a little higher than its usual alto timbre.

"Everyone back to the *Brigato* and don't take or touch anything. We're leaving."

No one argued as they headed out at the best speed possible without actually breaking into a run.

They were three hours away from the *Ghost* before Marlis finished decrypting the logs, and Zyra gleaned what information she needed from them. Severin came into their cabin as she was typing the message she would send to Kafka Rybar:

It is my difficult and grave duty to inform you of finding the ship Andromeda's Ghost *drifting in sector 4.35782. According to the logs, it was attacked by the pirate ship* Ravenger. *However, it is my belief those on board may have escaped. There was some sign of defense, and none of the bodies we discovered were of the* Ghost's *crew or passengers.*

"I thought you were going to record a holo message." Severin said, reading over the shoulders he rubbed absently.

"I am, but not without a script," she said. "Mmmm, that feels good." She closed her eyes and sighed.

"You going to tell him everything?"

She gave a mirthless laugh. "No! Let his own people find it and explain pirate ghosts to him." She returned to her message.

We have taken nothing from the ship except a copy of the log to be able to send full information to you. It is my hope this information will assist you in locating your kin.

She signed it Captain Zyra Quinn, *Brigato,* registration OSS64752, Orion Salvage Station. After a couple tweaks of editing, she recorded the final version and sent the data capsule on its way ahead of them. Data capsules automatically triggered the portal array at the jump point and traveled faster than any ship. The *Brigato* was nearly two days away from the array.

She walked to the bed and flopped down in exhaustion, her arm over her eyes. Severin, who was already under the coverlet, turned on his elbow, leaning his head on his hand.

"I thought I'd seen everything, Sev. How am I supposed to get those images out of my head?"

He reached over and pulled her into his arms.

"You don't, you just file them away as best you can, just like you always do. You can't say it wasn't what they deserved."

"True, but witch-cursed ghosts? That's a new one."

"There are psi witches," he said.

"Yes, but it's mind science. Telepathy and telekinesis," she said yawning, "not curses and ghosts." It took awhile, but she finally drifted to sleep in her husband's embrace.

Skreeee! Skreeee!

The alarm jolted Zyra and Severin hours later. Bare feet hit the floor before the coverlet did as jumpsuits were pulled on and fastened.

"We've got incoming, Captain," came Kag's voice from engineering. "And they don't look friendly."

Zyra and Alek hit the bridge at the same time. Alek jumped the rail, landing in his station as he punched in the commands to take the ship off auto pilot. Marlis arrived and slipped into the second station.

"How far?" Zyra asked.

"Twenty minutes," Marlis said. "Too fast for legit, and no transponder. Gotta be pirates."

"Damn. Out run them?"

"Not likely," said Alek. "We're still a day from the array, and they're between us and it."

"Hiding places, then." She tapped on her controls, and the display showed the system they were in. "How about these moons? Might be able to keep behind one."

"Worth a try. Send the distress beacon?"

"Hell, yes. I'm not proud. But system coordinates only; no homing signal. And sink some eyes."

The *Brigato* held position on the far side of the largest moon orbiting a nondescript gas giant. In this sector, planets had numbers rather than names since none were habitable. The sensors they'd shot into the opposite side of the moon showed the other ship slowing and scanning each moon.

The pirate ship bristled with weaponry and easily out massed the *Brigato* three times over.

"Close up there; it's got markings."

Marlis zoomed in on the area. A typical pirate skull but with manacles hanging from the crossed bones.

"Slavers," Alek said.

"Kag," Zyra called down, "keep those engines hot."

The pirate moved from one moon to the next, getting slowly closer to the one the *Brigato* hid behind.

"She's launching," Marlis said from the other console. "Drone to either side—we'll be found in five."

"Give me all you've got, Kag."

Alek hit the controls, and the g-forces pushed them back in their chairs. He climbed straight up as the drones rounded the moon's curve.

"Hope they aren't interested in a chase."

Alek opened the throttle full, and the engines whined in complaint. Surprise worked for a short while as the larger ship maneuvered away from the moons and the planet's gravity well, but the pirates began to gain on them far too soon. The bridge jolted as an enemy ordinance hit the starboard engine.

"There's another one coming in!" shouted Marlis.

Could this get any worse? Thought Zyra. *We are not worth fighting over!*

"In front of us. She's firing."

"Brace for impact!" Zyra called over the com.

The missiles closed, and Zyra held her breath, wondering how they were going to survive.

The impact was not the one she expected. The missiles passed by the *Brigato* and slammed into the slaver instead. Shock waves buffeted them, but nothing to cause damage.

The second ship closed on the slaver. Smaller, though still twice the *Brigato's* size, it expertly darted in to strike then was away on the other side before the pirates could react.

"Wow," Alek breathed. "Someday, I promise, if we live, I will be that good."

The ship's beams sliced into the pirate like swipes from a massive claw, additional missiles hitting every mark targeted. Before long the pirate was dead in space, shedding atmosphere, debris, and bodies.

The second ship swung around and glided smoothly up to face the *Brigato*.

"Cap'n," Alek said, astonished and pointing to the screen, which showed the name on the side of the other ship: *Ravenger*.

"They're hailing us," said Marlis.

"Open the channel," Zyra said, still trying to wrap her confused brain around what had just happened.

The screen came to life showing a woman in her twenties, auburn hair framing clear brown eyes in a face known throughout the system.

"I am Terezka Rybar, captain of the newly christened *Maiden's Revenge*. May we offer assistance, Captain Quinn?"

"Yes, certainly. And thank you. We're lucky you arrived when you did."

Terezka smiled. "Luck had nothing to do with it. May we board?"

"Of course, be welcome."

Terezka Rybar entered Zyra's small office, but she was not the giddy, high fashion socialite of the vids. This woman wore a jumpsuit not unlike Zyra's and exuded intelligence and serious capability. She was accompanied by her equally famous and unexpected sister. Terezka offered her hand, and Zyra accepted.

"Captain Quinn," Terezka said, "this is my sister, Nikala." Nikala's hair was darker and the eyes nearly black, but the resemblance was distinct. Rather than her hand, Nikala bowed, so Zyra returned it.

As they sat, Zyra poured tea. "I must admit, you're not what I expected."

Terezka smiled. "Our reputation is a carefully crafted fiction and has served its purpose. However, I am pleased to find yours is well deserved and honest."

Zyra acknowledged the compliment with a nod, then asked, "How is it your rescue was not lucky?"

"We were looking for you," said Nikala, "I read the missive to our father. We appreciate your delicacy and kindness."

"Read? A data capsule can't be read in flight."

Terezka smiled. "A level 10 psi-witch can scan it as it passes, even in hyperspace. My sister's level is," she paused, "well, considerably higher than 10."

"So that was your handiwork." Zyra directed the comment to Nikala.

"You disapprove?"

"While I can't say they didn't deserve it," Zyra said carefully, "it was rather extreme."

Terezka was solemn. "Our cousin Safi fell prey to that very crew two years ago." Terezka's voice was cold as space. "By the time my uncle found her, her mind was gone from the brutality she'd received. She was only thirteen. Considering the justice they deserved, we were lenient."

"But . . . ghosts?" Zyra couldn't help it; everything she knew said ghosts did not exist.

"They're psyches, if you will," said Nikala, "and yes, quite trapped unless I remove the barriers, which I won't. They're conscious minds, caught at the second before death and well aware of how much their existence has been limited."

"But ghosts make a much better story, don't you think?" Asked Terezka conversationally, taking a sip of tea. "And by all means, we want it told—what you found, what you saw inside. We expect the tale will spread, embellished as it is shared. All to our benefit."

Zyra put her cup down. "You're going to use that ship to hit pirates."

"Yes. When we're finished with our modifications, and repaint, we'll head for the Rim. By then we want our reputation preceding us, rumors to rattle every slaver captain and crew in the quadrant."

Zyra couldn't help grinning at the prospect of slavers getting a dose of real justice. "What about your father?"

"For now, your message is sufficient. In time, and through quiet channels, we will contact him. He will be proud."

"I'm sure he will," Zyra said, sincerely impressed. "Well, I don't know what it'll do to our credibility, but okay, we'll tell what we found, if that's what you want. No doubt there will be a few who will check it out for themselves."

"We're counting on it," Terezka said. "They'll find exactly what you found."

Zyra was relieved at their explanation; still she had to ask, "By the way, how did you manage the on and off cold on the Ghost?"

"Cold?" Nikala looked confused. "Wasn't the environmental working? We left it on."

Zyra swallowed, thankful her long-sleeved uniform hid the sudden goose bumps as a chill ran down her spine, but all she said was, "Just a glitch, I guess."

The com flashed, and Zyra answered. "How is it, Kag?"

"Their engineer is almost as good as me. Two hours tops."

"Sounds good." Then turning back to her guests. "I wish you good hunting. And again, I thank you for the rescue."

Late the next day, the *Brigato* pulled into Orion Salvage Yard with only the quarter full hold from the asteroid damaged vessel.

Zyra sat in front of the screen in her office and started pulling up the list of bills needing payment, mentally dividing them into categories of "must pay" and "beg for extension" and wondering if the *Ghost* story would be believed by her creditors.

She went from account to account. There had to be a glitch.

"This is not possible," she said out loud.

She paged back, refreshed and paged through again. Every bill that had been hanging over her head when she left dock was paid. Her insurance and port fees were paid five years in advance. And then . . .

"My God." She hardly breathed looking at the notice from the loan company of the paid in full note, accompanied by the cleared title to the *Brigato*!

She sat staring, bewildered and astonished, tears pooling in her eyes, blurring her vision. If this was an accounting glitch it was a cruel one. After wiping her eyes, she noticed the message light blinking on her screen and hit the button with a shaking hand. Terezka Rybar appeared on the screen.

"Hello, Captain Quinn. Consider this a down payment on our new reputation." The message closed and deleted itself. She'd never seen that happen before and for a moment just stared at the screen.

Zyra smiled slowly, then laughed out loud and spun in her chair with a whoop before hitting the com.

"Jupiter's Moonshine, one hour," she announced to the crew. "First round's on me. We've got a ghost story to tell!"

CONFLICTS OF CONSCIENCE

by
Cat Greenberg

This is a story about choosing between right and wrong, and all the gray areas you never prepared for, when one is faced with the unimaginable.

Shalin filled her mind with the sound of the surf crashing below as she turned her face from the corpse lying at her feet. She clenched her jaw against the bile rising in her throat and swore inwardly, digging sharp nails into her palms—she would not be sick again!

Pain and determination slowly overcame nausea. Harder to control was the gnawing guilt. She was a healer, a Restorer, oathbound never to harm even in defense of her own life. And now she had shattered her oath by killing not once, but three times!

Not for myself.

It was the one sane thought she could cling to in the chaos. Were it for only herself, she would have accepted death to keep her oath, but the invaders attacked her little sister and her mother. In shock she reacted with the only weapon she had—her Restorer's gift, the gift she had vowed never to use to kill.

It is not their Oath; how can it ask for their lives?

With a last shudder she steeled herself and turned back toward the man on the ground. Her throat was tight with the effort it took to ignore the shocked expression in his dead eyes, to not be reminded of the same rictus on the two in the keep above. She undid his sword belt and slid it out from under him. She pulled the dagger from his boot cuff, then rolled the body over the edge of the cliff.

"How did he find the hidden passage?" Her mother asked from behind. Shalin's sister, Althea, barely five years old, clung to her mother's skirt, staring wide-eyed at the ground where the dead man had lain.

"He didn't. He was pretty scraped up; I think he fell down the slope in the dark and was trying to find his way back up. Until we came out."

She handed her mother the sword belt. "Here, you might need this." She put the knife in her own boot cuff, thankful the Guild encouraged breeches.

Her mother gently disentangled Althea's grip as she put on the belt, tucking her skirts up into it.

"We have a few hours before dawn," Shalin said. "Let's make use of them."

The steep, rocky path down from the escape tunnel ledge was difficult to navigate in the dark. Several times the three slid as much as walked, scraping arms and legs on bare rocks and thorny branches. There were only three paths leading down to the beach, all deliberately camouflaged by overgrowth. Everywhere else the sheer face of cliffs had long protected Morvaine Holding from sea attacks. Those same cliffs would offer cover from above as they traveled along the beach.

Shalin's older brother, Kavan, lived in Caldean Holding, its western border a day's hard ride east on the main road. It would take two days to make it there on foot following the shoreline. Drinking water might be a problem, and the journey would not be pleasant, but it was survivable.

The morning found the three a good seven miles up the coast. Shalin pointed to a cave as they rounded a cliff bend, and they headed for it. Althea was asleep, carried on Shalin's back. As they entered, she gently lowered her little sister to her mother's lap before dropping to the sandy floor herself.

"No recent watermarks," Shalin said, studying the cave walls. "At least we won't have to worry about the tide washing us out in our sleep. We can start again when it gets dark."

For a little while, they just sat recovering.

"Mother," Shalin's soft words echoed faintly in the small cavern. "They wore Ansgar livery underneath ours. I wouldn't have believed they'd be that bold. Has it gotten so bad?"

"We didn't think so. Lady Katla has been particularly persistent lately, but I never expected outright attack." She sighed. "So much for your first visit home from the Guild."

"Not quite the welcoming committee I expected."

Ansgar, their northern neighbor, had always been envious of Morvaine's ancient ties to Caldean and the large river mouth port Morvaine helped them manage and protect.

"They will come after us," her mother said flatly.

"For the Lady of the Hold and two of the three heirs?" Shalin asked sardonically. "Oh yes, they will come after us. Our best hope is they may think lastly of our current route. Kavan can't know what's happened, else there would be swarms of Caldean forces here, and Ansgar will not want to attract his attention while we are yet at large."

Althea stirred, silencing the women. Their discussion would only confuse and upset her more than the journey already did.

"I'm hungry, Mama."

"I know. We all are. I'm sorry."

Talkative Althea was unusually quiet, and Shalin worried about her little sister. Shock could do a lot of damage, even to the normally resilient child mind. Althea clung to mother's arm in an iron grip, eyes dark and haunted. Shalin moved over and put her hand on the girl's forehead.

Peace, she sent, and sleep, going deep as she would have a patient needing surgery, sending Althea into a quiet, dreamless sleep.

Her mother smiled as Althea relaxed. "At least one of us will get some rest."

"Well, we're going to have to try. We should be safe enough for today."

As she lay down, Shalin cast her mind out along the road at the top of the cliffs. No pursuers as yet. First, they would thoroughly search Morvaine Hold. Morvaine sprawled upwards, having been added onto for generations. It was a delight for every child born there, with level upon level of hidden alcoves and passages for exploring and pretend adventures. It would take time, but Shalin knew as soon as they began an outside search their chances of escape slimmed considerably. She could only hope the delay would be enough for them to reach Caldean.

Shalin took a deep breath and reached out further. The last time they'd seen her father, he was surrounded but holding his own against four attackers. He had shouted to her, "Get them out!" and Shalin obeyed. Now she reached out for her father's familiar presence, fearing she'd find nothing.

No, wait— he was alive!

He was injured, his mind filled with the effort of controlling his pain. Thoughts colored with worry, mingled with hope. He knew they were still free. She withdrew, too exhausted to hold the contact.

"Mother, he's alive. Father's still alive."

She heard the sob in her mother's relieved sigh.

They had to reach Kavan.

Shalin woke with a start as the nightmare images slithered back into their dark corners. It was dusk outside; they could leave soon. She looked over at her mother and was not surprised to see her awake and looking back. She smiled reassuringly, and Shalin tried to smile back. Althea was curled like a kitten against her mother, still asleep.

"I had nightmares, too," her mother said, then paused. "Shalin," she continued slowly, "I want you to know how grateful I am that you were there for us. I know the pain it must cause you, but . . ."

"Please, Mother," Shalin interrupted. Her throat tightened, and she looked away.

"Look at me, daughter. Do not be ashamed by what you did to save us. You had no choice."

"I'm not. I'm supposed to feel shame, but I don't. Regret at what I had to do, yes; guilt because I did it so easily, but not shame." She got up and walked to the mouth of the cave, staring at the sunset sea. She turned back to her mother, shaking her head. "My vows are broken. I cannot change that. But your safety is more important. It is enough for now. If we don't reach Kavan in time, it won't matter what I feel."

They left as soon as it was full dark. The moon was a wide crescent when it rose, adding just enough light to see the dim shapes of rock and debris directly in front of them without being bright enough to give them away from above. Should someone look down from the cliff, the three would be lost in the mottled shadows.

The shoreline became rockier, and they picked their way more carefully. Weakened by a day without food or water also slowed them.

"My tummy hurts," Althea whimpered as they rested, waiting for the tide to finish receding.

"I know, sweeting," her mother soothed. She looked at Shalin, "Is there anything you can do?"

"I could ease the pain of the cramping some," she said. "It won't last long, maybe an hour or two."

Her mother nodded, then added "Wait, will it weaken you?"

"A little, but I can manage."

The tide finished, and they inched their way around a jutting cliff whose base was just barely out of the water even at low tide. The shoreline to Caldean was treacherous. A few feet into the water, and the shelf of land fell off precipitously, where the drag of the tide could drown even a strong swimmer. They managed to make it all but the last couple of miles before the first light of predawn made them search out another cave.

Shalin again sent out her awareness before they slept and found a band of men on the main road near Morvaine Keep. The outside search was on. There were two villages and several farms along the east road toward Caldean, which would be searched first. She doubted it would take them all day. The second village had a trail wide enough for horses to manage, leading down to the beach, but once on the beach they would soon be as much on foot as the fugitives—horses simply don't climb boulders.

Shalin's first impulse was to keep going, but exhaustion threatened as much as their pursuers, and navigating the shoreline was already difficult enough.

"Mother, it's not safe to sleep today."

"You have seen them?"

Shalin nodded. "We have an hour or two at most if we're to stay ahead of them."

"Then we'd better get what rest we can."

It was nearing midday when Shalin spotted the Caldean sea flag, waving like a flaring beacon at the top of the cliffs. They were almost safe.

Almost.

Shalin heard the shout from above as they were climbing the last group of jagged rocks before reaching clear beach. About a quarter mile behind, a lone horseman stood on the edge of the cliff. She looked back down the shoreline to where the man directed his shouts and saw the party on foot.

"Take Althea and run as fast as you can, Mother. Get past the flag and as far into Caldean as you can go. Find a village, a farm—anything! I'll hold them off as long as I can."

"Shalin, no. Come with us." The pained look in her mother's eyes was almost too much. "They'll kill you."

"Trust me, please. I have no intention of letting them get that close. Go," she pleaded, "for Althea's sake."

Her mother looked from the men to Shalin, then to the cliff and back.

"I love you," she said finally, touching her daughter's cheek. She was reluctant and clearly unconvinced, but she scooped up Althea.

"I love you, too," she touched Althea's tear streaked face, "both of you. I will see you soon."

Her mother turned and left, moving as fast as the terrain would let them. Her little sister's wide, terrified gaze gripped her heart like a fist of ice and she turned angrily back to the hunters.

"You've no right to hunt us! To terrorize my sister!" she cried wildly. "I could kill you from here, all of you!"

What was she saying? Her vows truly were shattered if this was how she thought of life now, even their lives.

She closed her eyes a moment, taking deep, measured breaths. Not this time, not deliberately. She opened her eyes again.

"No," she said quietly, "I won't let you push me to break my vows again! There has to be another way."

She climbed onto the highest boulder, hoping it would distract the horseman from her mother's flight, and studied the cliff and beach. The tide was nearly in. Could that help? Yes, they were already wading hip deep between the narrow strip of rocks. The cliffs towered above them, overhanging in spots. If she could just delay them or push them further into the water. The waves were getting quite strong, and the danger of undertow where the land fell off would not be known to them.

She smiled. Those trees will do. They were large and growing at one of those impossible angles scrub trees sometimes do, hanging just ahead and above the band of men.

Shalin concentrated on the sand and dirt holding the trees in place. She felt deep into the structure, as she would have a wound, moving aside the ground that held it in place, the same as she would have moved a bone to set it, then began weakening the roots, severing the strands one by one. Her sides were slick with sweat, and she was shaking with effort when at last the trees released their hold and came crashing down in front of the men, bringing a cascade of sand, dirt, and rocks with them as they fell. The men were thrown backward by the falling debris. Some tried wading farther out, only to be grabbed by the undertow or tossed like flotsam in the crashing waves.

The band in complete chaos, she looked up at the horseman, now directly above her, raising her fist in defiance as she recognized Lady Katla's son glaring down at her.

Abelard spurred his horse farther along the cliff, disappearing from sight.

He was looking for a way to cut her off. He was going to find the path she knew was not much farther down the road. Shalin's route was shorter, but the rocks slowed her down. It was a race to see if she could scramble faster than his horse could run. Rock finally gave way to clear beach, and she broke into a dead run. Her mother and sister were past the flag, out of sight. Not more than fifty feet before she'd have reached safety, Abelard emerged on the beach in front of her. His sword drawn, he sat his foaming and blowing horse casually, waiting. Shalin stopped just out of his reach.

"So," he said, "the Restorer who kills." She froze. Of course, he knew. What other explanation was there for dead men without a mark on them? "You've cost me good men." His smile chilled more than the sea breeze. "Still, you could be very useful to us. Mother will be so pleased when I bring you back."

"If you bring me back. Unless you're stupid enough to think I'll come willingly."

"Not even to save your father?"

"My father would rather die than watch me acquiesce to an invader."

"Perhaps. I am sure we will have the opportunity to test your theory in some entertaining way."

"Aren't you afraid you'll meet the same fate as your men?"

His cold smile was back as she inched her way toward the water's edge.

"No, not at all. Since I am not dead yet, I can only surmise you had no choice before; besides you weren't saving yourself. No, I don't think you will kill me, because this time it would be your choice."

Abelard walked his horse in front of her, mirroring her pacing path to the water, then back toward the cliff again.

"You'll never get past me," he was irritatingly amused. "And if you do, I'm sure Garth here," he patted the horse's neck, "can outrun you—even on sand."

"Stalemate, then."

The smile was gone. "I'm not a patient man. Nor will I be gentle if you don't come quietly."

He was right. She wouldn't choose to break her vow now that the only threat was to herself. But, while kindness was always encouraged, her vow of no harm did not extend to animals.

She started edging toward the water again. This time as he moved to cut her off, his horse danced, agitated.

"Easy, Garth. What are you doing?" he demanded.

She silently apologized to the beast, then reached to the muscles in his withers, making them spasm painfully. Garth whinnied, danced sideways, bucking and rearing. Abelard grabbed at the reins and pommel to keep from falling, but his sword was knocked from his hand to drop point down in the sand as he hopelessly tried to control his mount. Shalin darted in as the horse danced closer to the water; she grabbed

104

the sword by the hilt and ran up the beach, staying on the more solid wet sand. One more twinge to the horse, this time a sharp stab to the sacral vertebrae, and Garth bucked violently. The heir to Ansgar was thrown free, landing with a splash in the surf.

Shalin paused to fling the sword far into the water and saw a huge wave knock Abelard down just as he was trying to rise.

She ran full speed for the flag and never looked back again. She heard shouts as she climbed toward the bluff. Looking up, she was relieved to see Caldean colors. Her mother had made it.

It was mid-afternoon the next day when word came from Kavan of the liberation of the Lord of Morvaine. Lady Katla managed to escape, retreating to her own lands, but Abelard was a prisoner of Caldean.

"It's over," Shalin whispered to herself, knowing what must come next. She tried to slip out quietly, but her mother caught her as she reached the main doors.

"Not even a goodbye? Where are you going, Shalin?"

She looked at her mother, confused by the question. Surely, she knew where Shalin must go.

"Back to Blackburough," she said flatly. "I have broken my vows by killing three men and must submit myself to the Guild I am no longer worthy to claim as my own." The ritual words sounded dead and remote.

"Why?" Her mother demanded, grabbing her arm and forcing Shalin to turn and look at her. "Because of an oath requiring you to no longer be human?" Her mother's sudden fury jolted Shalin out of her daze.

"I have to." She didn't want to argue; this was going to be hard enough as it was.

"No, you don't. There's no proof it was you. Abelard will have no one to tell his accusations to. We do not have to tell anyone it was you who struck the blows."

Shalin stepped back, incredulous. "You make it sound as though I killed them with a sword! That would have been bad enough. My mind reached into their hearts and stopped them from beating. I used my gift to kill!"

"You also used it to save, Shalin. You could have killed the hunting party, and Abelard, but you didn't. When you had the choice and the time to think, you didn't harm those who wished us harm. Will you punish yourself for instincts? We would be dead or in the hands of Ansgar if you had not acted as you did. Do you really think yourself unworthy of the work you were born to do?" She took Shalin's hands in hers. "Say nothing, Shalin," she begged. "No one will ever know."

The pain and pleading in her mother's eyes were a knife to her heart. "They already do, mother."

Shalin opened the doors. A man and woman wearing Guild colors were crossing the courtyard.

"How?" her mother breathed.

"Restorers cannot hide things. Our minds are always open to one another at a subconscious level. The others knew as soon as it happened."

They stood in silence, watching the two approach. They were older than her mother, and the sigillary they wore named them Grand Masters. When they reached the steps, they bowed to the Lady of Morvaine, then turned to Shalin.

"Restorer Shalin, you are hereby summoned to the Restorer Guild Consulate in Blackburough to answer the charge of oathbreaking. Will you submit?"

"I will submit."

"No! She did it to save us, not herself! Doesn't that count for anything?" Her mother protested.

"Mother, please." Then she turned to the Masters. "I'm sorry, this is very hard for her. It has been a trying few days."

"Lady Adeenna," the woman addressed Shalin's mother kindly, "the circumstances of the incident are known to the Guild and will be taken under advisement. It does not, cannot, change the severity of the offense. The Guild Elders will decide her fate."

The Lady of Morvaine would not be placated.

"Tell me, Guild Master, would you have allowed your mother and little sister to be killed, or worse, if it had been you?"

It was the man who answered.

"Would you undo two hundred years of sacrifice? Would you have us once again hunted and burned as witches by those who fear our abilities? The forming of the Guild and enforcement of the Oath were the only way we could be free to use our gifts. Would you ask the undoing of all the trust we have built for one person?"

"No," said Shalin, and when her mother started to open her mouth to argue, "No!" Then to the Guild Masters, "May I have a moment with my mother?" They bowed and walked to wait by the gate.

"What will they do to you?" her mother asked.

She gave a small ironic chuckle. "Well, they can't kill me, if that's your worry. I will likely be required to renounce my position as a Restorer, and they will strip me of all Guild affiliation. The removal of the Guild sigil on the back of my hand will leave a scar that will brand me, making me an outcast in every respectable Hold and village of the Five Lands."

"No, not all. You will never be an outcast in Morvaine. Will you come home? It won't be safe for you without the protection of the Guild sigil."

"Eventually, but not right away. The punishment will satisfy the Guild, but it won't cleanse me. I need to find some penance, for myself. I have heard rumors of remote places within the Five Lands that are too poor to send for a Guild Restorer. I believe it shames the Guild that this is so. Once, I thought perhaps I could work to correct the oversights within the Guild. Now I'll try to do it outside the Guild. I will search for them, help if I can. Perhaps they will not mind a disgraced Restorer. An outcast helping the outcast. It will let me keep my vows in my heart, even if they are recognized by no one else."

Her mother pulled her close. "You are more worthy of your vows than anyone I have ever known. I am now, and always shall be, proud of you."

They held each other for a long time before Shalin disentangled herself, trying to keep tears at bay, knowing neither wanted to admit how long it might be before they saw each other again, if ever.

"I have to go."

"Fair journey, my daughter," her mother said and kissed Shalin's brow.

Shalin turned and walked to the gate where the Grand Masters waited, falling into step behind them as the three passed through in silence.

LESSONS
IN THE DARK
by
Cat Greenberg

*This is one of two stories in this
anthology that are reprints of stories
that originally appeared in* Marion
Zimmer Bradley's Fantasy Magazine
*and were written under my previous
name, Sandra C. Morrese. This one
appeared in Issue 16 in the spring of
1992.*

The battle became endless. Bodies
rose and fell before her in a scarlet blur
of unceasing violence. How long like
this? Her sword came up and spilled an
enemy's blood in the downstroke. He
was replaced by another.

We are sorely outnumbered, she
thought. *In the end we shall all have our
turn on their blades.*

Yet she continued, and her employer's foes continued to die.

She saw the blow coming. As it came crashing down, a distant part of her mind slowed and acknowledged that she could not deflect this one. But she knew that her opponent, too, would fall. Her head exploded with the burning pain of his blade, but she managed to complete her turn, felt her own blade slice flesh, and saw the surprised agony on his face. Then she saw nothing but spinning darkness and blessed oblivion.

Five-year-old Gara sat on the edge of the straw pallet she shared with her mother, watching her ready herself for yet another fight.

"Mama," she said seriously. "Why don't you call Freedom Challenge? Carak says you have more than enough wins."

Isa stopped and looked at her daughter. Then she knelt and clasped both of Gara's hands in hers. "Because I will not leave you," she said earnestly.

Twelve-year-old Gara swung again and again at the bells, each strike strong and precise. "Good. Excellent," called the old trainer, Carak. "At this rate, you will exceed even your own mother."

Fourteen-year-old Gara stood in the doorway, tears threatening to break through her tight control as she again watched her mother dress for the arena. This would be Isa's last fight. Gara felt it in her bones, knew it as she'd known about old Carak's heart last spring. She ached with the need to tell her but couldn't get the words past her tightening throat. Telling her wouldn't change anything, but it might alter her performance and make the death blow Gara saw less quick, so she kept silent. Isa turned and signed victory for the last time. Gara returned it, somehow managing to smile.

Nineteen-year-old Gara stood in the center of the arena, her bloody sword raised and her foot on the chest of her dead opponent—Freedom Challenge met. She matched the gaze of her master and held it as he declared her release—the same master who'd sent her mother into the ring time and again until she no longer returned. Hate burned in her mind as he recited the formal words that made her a free citizen. She'd lowered her sword and turned when he clutched his chest in pain and slumped over in his chair. It was later, in the slave compound as she packed what few things she now owned, that she learned he was dead.

Gara's mind swam and tumbled its way to a fuzzy consciousness. She lay still as her head cleared more, taking in all she could of her surroundings without giving away her lucid state. She could feel bandages across her eyes, impossible to open them. The battle came back to her, and she remembered the blow to her skull. By her own calculations, she should be dead. Mercenary's luck, she supposed. But where was she?

She was lying in a bed, that was plain. Strange, since the camp healer's tent had none. And where was the battle noise? She strained her ears but heard only a distant and indistinguishable blend of sounds. And closer, soft breathing. Someone sat beside her.

Asleep? Impossible to tell. A guard? Surely her employer's enemies would not have bound her wounds so carefully or put her anywhere but the floor of a crowded cell. She was not high enough in rank to be of any importance to them. She knew how to fight and did so. Secrets were given to others.

She listened carefully for several more minutes. The breathing remained steady and quiet, no other movement, so she decided to venture a hand to her face to check the extent of her injuries.

Her hand would not move. She felt the straps restraining both arms, and her legs, too. An unfamiliar fear shot through the pit of her stomach. She'd been a warrior more years than she cared to count and had faced battle death a thousand times over; but to be captured, blind and unable to move. . . . Never had she felt so totally helpless.

She took a deep breath, forcing down the surge of panic. She strained carefully against the straps. They wouldn't loosen. On second thought, she was surprised at how comfortably they'd been placed. If she hadn't moved, she wouldn't have noticed them. Then she heard movement beside her.

"You are awake," a woman's voice addressed her. She sounded older than Gara by many years, but the voice was soft with its age rather than harsh.

"Good, good," the woman continued and laid a hand on each of Gara's cheeks, then briefly slipped it under Gara's neck.

"Ah!" the unseen presence proclaimed. "The fever's broken now. Here, let me loosen the bonds. You were quite a handful in that fever of yours; we feared you might harm yourself."

Gara felt the restrains lifted, first off her legs, then her arms. Loosed, she sat up quickly, grabbing the older woman's wrist in a grip that barely kept from breaking it. Then her head began to spin violently.

"No, no, no," the other woman said in gentle admonishment. Gara could feel no fear in the woman, something that surprised even her dull and dizzy senses.

"You must not get up so quickly," the woman continued. "You are not yet ready." Her voice was full of concern, confusing Gara even more. "Here, lie back again."

Gara released her hold, unable to remain upright. The woman eased her back down on the bed.

"Who are you?" Gara managed to ask after the spinning slowed. Her voice cracked with disuse.

Silence. Then, "A helper. We serve the Goddess Iole, Mother of the Dawn, and help all who come to our door."

"But how did I come here? I don't remember being able to walk."

"You weren't. You were found on the field and brought here."

"Who won?"

"The war? Does it matter so? It is over, and you are here."

"But where is this place? It sounds very large. But there were no large structures near the battlefield."

"So many questions!" the woman exclaimed, fussing with Gara's blanket and tucking her in like a small child. "You should rest now. Surely your questions can wait until you are stronger." The woman touched Gara's cheek lightly.

Gara wanted to protest but felt her brain fogging over again.

"Yes," the invisible woman soothed, "sleep now, rest, rest . . . " The words faded into the dark.

Gara swam back to the surface, fighting her way up as though through quicksand. Battle dreams and long forgotten memories faded, returning to the void she'd long ago banished them to. Once more she lay there, blind but awake, and listened. This time no sounds seemed near her. She raised her hands a little and let out a slow relieved breath, finding them free this time. She touched the bandages. They covered her head and face down to her nose. She pressed gingerly along her forehead, locating the wound, which should have killed her. It stretched from the middle of her forehead to below her right temple by the feel of it. The sword must not have hit true or it would surely have split her skull.

She pushed herself ever so slowly up onto her elbows. Her head remained quiet, so she brought herself carefully upright. A dull ache began but her equilibrium stayed, so she ventured one leg over the edge, then the other. She sat for a moment, listening and making sure she wouldn't topple over again.

She felt along the edge of the bed as she sat there. The bed was large. It had a thick wooden frame and was higher than she'd expected. She eased herself to the floor, and her bare toes sank into the deep pile of a luxurious fur rug.

What kind of place is this? With wooden beds and carpets and healers who don't immediately ask for payment and the name of your employer?

She turned and rifled through the blankets for any sign of her clothing. Nothing. Just the undertunic she wore. The room was chilly, so she wrapped the blanket about her shoulders. She felt her way toward the headboard. It was elaborately carved. The luxury puzzled her. She extended her arms and spread her hands out before her, one high and one low. She took several careful steps before her fingers encountered the cool stone of the wall. It was wide and smooth with age and use, and in her mind she envisioned a massive keep surrounded by a tall stone wall.

But there were none near the battlefield, she thought. *Where am I?*

Footsteps and the sound of a latch opening caught her attention, and she turned toward the sound. Two sets of footsteps entered.

"I told you she would be up and walking," said the voice of her caregiver.

"Yes," said a new voice. "You are feeling better, child?"

Did Gara imagine a smile in that silken voice? She felt compelled to trust, as though she'd know this woman all her life.

"My head aches," she replied slowly, trying hard to regain the suspicious nature that had kept her alive this long, "but at least it is still attached." Both older women chuckled softly. "Thank you for your help."

"You are most welcome, but thanks are not necessary. It is the Dawn Mother's work we do and gladly. I am Aurell, the High Priestess here, and I believe you have many questions."

"Y- yes, I do."

"Come, let us talk. Galene, bring her some breakfast. She must be famished."

Gara heard the caregiver leave. "Come, child, sit."

Gara moved across the room toward the voice, finding a stuffed chair by the hearth. The High Priestess stirred the coals and added several pieces of wood until it blazed warm before them. Gara listened to the woman's movements until she heard her seat herself in an equally soft chair across from Gara.

"Now then," the woman said, "what do you wish to know?"

Gara paused so the questions wouldn't all tumble out at once and tried to order her thoughts. "Where am I?" she asked finally.

"The Convent of Iole, Mother Dawn."

"You are all priestesses?"

"We all serve Our Lady in whatever office we are able to."

"Where is this place?"

"Roughly two days' ride east of the field where you were found."

Gara's mouth dropped open. How could she have survived such a journey?

"By the grace of our good Mother Dawn, many things are possible."

"But why me? I am only a fighter and of no importance to anyone."

"All are important to our Mother Iole. It is Her will that brought you here." Aurell did not continue about that. "Ah, here is Galene now. We will talk again after you have eaten."

A table was pulled in front of her, and the most tantalizing smells reached Gara from the tray they placed before her. Gara had thought eating blind would be difficult, but she quickly devoured the sweet breads, eggs, and fruit. Even the water tasted wonderful to Gara's deprived senses. She couldn't remember a better meal in her whole life.

After she finished, Gara saw Aurell smile. No . . . she imagined it; how could she see with her eyes covered?

"Are you better now? How does your head feel?"

"Yes, much better. When can the bandages come off?"

Aurell considered a moment, then reached over and lightly touched Gara's head.

"Three more days, I think."

"Will . . . " Gara paused and took a deep breath. "Will I be able to see?"

Aurell sat back in her chair and smiled again.

"Oh yes," she said with a strange note in her voice that puzzled Gara. "You will see better than you ever have."

Gara let out the breath she'd been holding. Fighting was all she knew, and if she were blinded . . . She'd seen crippled former mercenaries on city streets. Proud men and women brought to degradation, begging or selling their bodies when they could no longer sell their swords. She'd sworn to take her own life before she ever lived like that.

Gara and Aurell talked frequently over the next three days, although she was sometimes puzzled by the answers the older woman gave. Aurell's voice gave no hint of her years, yet Gara pictured her as being even older than Galene. She supposed it was Aurell's quiet, confident manner that made her think that.

She was allowed short walks, which gradually became longer. At first she thought it strange that they never took her hand, but rather walked just ahead of her, apparently trusting her to follow their voices and footsteps, although they were often silent. She was getting very good at it by the third day and had a reasonable idea of what the convent's layout was.

She was sitting in the garden after the midday meal when Aurell and Galene came to her. Gara looked toward them as they walked silently up.

"Well, you found the garden by yourself today," Galene said in greeting.

"Good afternoon, Galene, High Priestess." Gara nodded to each. "I hope you don't mind."

"Not at all," Aurell asured her. "I am pleased to see it."

"It is time to remove the bandages, Gara," Galene said.

Gara smiled. It was amazing how much she'd begun to smile lately.

"Can we do it here?"

"Here is fine," said Aurell, sitting down beside Gara as Galene began unwrapping cloth. After the last bandage was pulled away, Gara slowly opened her eyes, then froze.

"I'm still blind!" she half screamed as wild terror flooded through her. "You said I would see, but I am blind!"

Aurell grasped Gara's hands firmly, and she felt her panic ebb a little.

"You have *never* been blind. I said you would see, not that your eyes would be saved. Think, child. Do you not see me? Do you not see the flowers that surround you? Do you not know the shape of the convent?"

Gara calmed, distracted from her terror.

"I . . . I don't understand."

"You have a gift, child. One you have never realized you had, though it has aided you your whole life. You have even killed with it. Your slave master did not die by accident the day you were freed."

Gara was taken aback.

"How do you know this? I told you nothing of my years as a gladiator."

"Our Lady has watched over you for many years until circumstances could bring you to Her. It was She who suspended time itself so that you could be brought safely to us. And since you first awoke, have you not seen, in your mind, this convent, us, the gardens?"

"I . . . can imagine . . . but . . . "

"You do not imagine; you *see* all that surrounds you. Where is Galene now?"

Without thinking, Gara pointed behind Aurell.

"How did you know that? She made no sound moving there."

"I . . . can . . . see her," Gara said hesitantly. "But I am only a mercenary. Without eyes . . . "

"Without eyes, you must seek another calling," Aurell said gently. "Perhaps even the one you were meant for all along."

This time, Gara *knew* the High Priestess smiled.

THE SUBSTANCE OF SHADOW

by
Cat Greenberg

This story started out as "Silhouette" when I was a guest at a con that wanted a story to put in the program book. Years later, after a major rewrite, it became "The Substance of Shadow." I offer it as a free download on the website but also decided to include it here.

Anyi faced the wind, tears drying on her cheeks, storm clouds roiling above the trees.

Tollan's storm.

She closed her eyes and breathed deeply, filling herself with the scent of the building tempest. Tornados of long, gray hair whipped about her head. Lightning leapt from cloud to cloud as thunder shook the ground.

She opened her eyes, power burning in them as she walked toward Dead Hill and justice.

The wind changed direction, pushing her forward, her hair blowing past her face, a standard flying at the head of a one-woman army. As she trudged higher up the barren hill, the wind surrounded her and helped her stay upright when knees long past their prime threatened to give out. Rain began halfway up, a steady stream of water. She reached the summit, panting, steeling herself for the task at hand. She straddled the ground on her knees, the wind buffeting her on all sides as the rain softened its attack.

There was no sense of time as she scooped and molded the form before her, arms covered with muddy clay. She flinched when lightning struck the ground nearby, sending bits of dirt spraying into the air around her. The storm grew impatient, but Anyi could not rush. The form must be exact, a complete and perfect duplicate of Tollan's form, the shadow of his Silhouette given substance.

The wind blew from all directions at

once; the lightning became so constant it mimicked the sun in brilliance, although it left the world as stark and drained of color as Anyi was drained of joy. The body finished, she began to smooth the head. Closing her eyes, she saw Tollan's face again: his sun-bronzed skin, the hint of a smile that always lingered, the love in his deep brown eyes.

New streaks of tears poured down her clay-smudged cheeks. She would never again see her soul reflected in those beautiful eyes—eyes that had lifelessly stared up at her from the floor of his workshop. Her grief wailed at the storm as she desperately tried to blot out the image.

She'd arrived home as dusk fell and caught but a glimpse of the cloaked figures fleeing into the woods. With a puzzled sense of dread, she'd run to her husband's workshop. She fell to her knees in the doorway, her heart nearly bursting as it hammered in her chest. Her beloved husband's body was tied to his chair, his head on the floor beside it with the villains' gag still stuffed in his mouth.

They must have surprised him. He was never one to set any but the most minimal wards, not wanting to risk harm to an innocent visitor. The only ward Tollan did use told him when visitors arrived and identified who they were. Strangers could not have caught him so off guard—which meant it was someone Tollan knew! With his hands tied and his mouth gagged, he could not make the incantations that would have saved his life.

As Anyi had wept, raging at the injustice of not knowing where to direct her vengeance, the Heartstone Tollan gave her thirty-five years ago on their Promise Day began to warm and pulse where it hung between her breasts. Thunder began to mutter in the distance as Tollan's essence pulsed within the stone and his soul whispered instructions. Anyi's magecraft was the gentler earth magics, nothing that would aid in bringing foes to justice. But Tollan had been an Archmage of the highest order, and as the storm grew, the knowledge of what she must do blossomed in Anyi's mind like a flower opening to the morning sun.

His assailants believed that by taking a sorcerer's head, you stole his power. Only Masters and Mistresses of the Guild knew the tale was a skillfully crafted lie. A wizard's power lay not in his head, but in his heart. With Tollan's death, his resided in the Heartstone worn by the person he trusted most: his partner and wife.

Anyi's eyes opened, and she gazed with grim satisfaction at the finished clay form; then she reached under her hair and unclasped the chain holding Tollan's Heartstone. The lightning drew closer as the words of incantation filled her mind.

"Form of clay, receive thy Master's heart," she said as she laid the amulet carefully on the form's chest and clasped the chain around its neck. "The Storm of Justice calls you to service. Elements of Earth and Air grant you leave to avenge thy Master's honor."

There was no other option available to her and Tollan. In exchange for their autonomy, crimes against a wizard, rare though they were, did not fall into any magistrate's jurisdiction. The Guild controlled its own by whatever means it deemed necessary. With the nearest Guild outpost a three day ride away, this clay Silhouette was their only recourse.

She stumbled back in the gusting wind. The Heartstone's glow pulsed in a dazzling synchronicity with each burst of lightning, the thunder an endless cacophony. One blinding flash struck the amulet directly, and she brought her arms up to shield her eyes. Deafening silence told Anyi that all was finished. She lowered her arms to see the clay Silhouette standing before her, mist rising from it, the amulet glowing with the power of her husband's heart.

She stepped aside to let it pass, then followed. Anyi hadn't seen their faces, but Tollan knew who his assassins were, and his spirit would guide the Silhouette. They thought themselves safe and unseen. They were wrong.

It was already past midnight; Anyi had only until dawn to find her husband's killers. The sun's first rays would carry her beloved Tollan's heart to the Beyond, and the Silhouette would again be formless clay.

Anyi followed as Tollan's Silhouette plodded purposefully toward the village, and her stomach soured. Ten years she and Tollan had called Mabina home. Ten years! They'd believed the people of the village cared about them and valued their service, thought of them as neighbors and friends. When their farms suffered from drought, Tollan and Anyi brought the rain. When little Tanika became lost, trapped in a sinkhole in the woods, it was Tollan's magecraft that found and rescued her. People came to her and Tollan time and again for the treatment of fevers, difficult births, even simple rashes; never was anyone turned away unaided, even when the only payment that could be offered was heartfelt thanks. It made Anyi sick to think someone whom they'd trusted, who perhaps had even guested at their table, could commit this obscene betrayal.

They passed through the village square, then turned left. Anyi stayed alert for any sign that their passage was observed, but all seemed peaceful in the warm summer night. The chirp of crickets, the trill of a night bird's song, and the flap of a bat's wing all drifted—so deceptively normal—past

Anyi. Only the gentle thump-shuffle the heavy, clay figure made as it walked was different from the sounds heard the previous evening when she'd strolled along these very roads for pleasure, Tollan at her side, holding her hand and laughing at the antics of two stray kittens. Tonight her companion was an eyeless clay form, shadow image of the man taken from her.

A dog came running out of an alley, prepared to bark, but instead it stopped and sat down, watching them pass in silence. Animals know when not to interfere.

They passed the last house, and still the figure shuffled on. Anyi glanced around frantically. Were her husband's killers foreigners? How could they have surprised him? Yet the Silhouette continued its passage out of the village and down the road. Unless—Anyi's heart sank with the thought—perhaps they were now fleeing on horseback. If so, she would never catch them before dawn.

Trees closed in around them as the road narrowed. Anyi could hear the rush of the river as they headed for North Road Fording. Could the Silhouette cross water? She wasn't sure. What knowledge she'd gained came from Tollan's spirit so she could make the Silhouette properly. With the task completed, it trickled from her memory like water from a leaky bucket.

Then she heard laughter; someone sat camped by the river! As they grew closer, the voices became clear over the rush of the water.

"Did you see the look on his face?" A female voice crowed. "He never dreamed I could do it. Hah!"

Anyi caught herself on the trunk of a tree and barely managed to keep from being sick. What kind of monster could exult in killing her gentle Tollan?

"Will you be quiet?" a younger male voice hissed. Both voices sounded familiar to Anyi, but in her grief-fogged mind she couldn't place them.

"Why?" Demanded the woman. "Having second thoughts?"

"You said you wanted to talk. You didn't say you were going to kill him!"

"Well now, lad, 'twas for your own good. You'd never have gone along if I'd told you. You should thank me," the voice sneered. "He would never have given you all his knowledge. None of them do! They just use you, then throw you away. But I beat them at their own game. Now the wizard's power is mine!"

"Is it?" demanded the boy. "Do you feel any different? All I feel is sick. Sick that I let you talk me into this, that I didn't see what you were going to do. He was my friend, and I betrayed him. How will I ever be able to face Mistress Anyi?" His voice broke then. "She will never forgive me. Never."

No! It was impossible. How could Gaelen be involved?

Tollan's sixteen-year-old apprentice was supposed to be visiting his family in Bevyn. They'd treated him like a son these past four years. And who was the other familiar voice, the gloating, laughing one?

"So? What can the wife of a dead wizard do? The power will come; I know it will. I took his head. The power of Archmage Tollan is mine! And you had better keep your wits about you, or you'll be the first one I use it on!"

Tollan's Silhouette emerged from the trees then, Anyi following. Her breath caught when she saw the laughing speaker.

"Rordyn!"

She'd come to her husband five years ago, asking to be apprenticed to Tollan. At fifteen, they'd thought her rather old to be a beginning apprentice, but they took her in anyway, and Tollan tested her. Rordyn held some talent, but her impatience and volatile temper made her a poor apprentice. Study of the craft is arduous and requires self-discipline and a temperate nature the girl could not manage. After only a month, Tollan sent Rordyn on her way. He'd been as gentle as possible, giving the lass more than a month's wages as severance and a letter of reference so she could apprentice in some other, nonmagical, profession. Rordyn tore up the letter and threw it at Tollan in disgust, swearing she would be a wizard, and if Tollan wouldn't teach her, someone else would. It was a year before they heard the rumors among the mage circles. The explanation for the girl's age was that she had already failed with three other wizards before Tollan.

Rordyn and Gaelen stood frozen at the sight of Anyi and the clay figure, not quite comprehending what they were facing. Cold rage burned in Anyi as she confronted Rordyn. "How dare you so much as speak his name!" Anyi screamed. "You should have accepted my husband's counsel. You are not suited to magic and never will be!"

Rordyn drew herself up, brandishing a sword. "I will be a wizard this night. Do you not recognize your dear husband's blood? I took his head. His power is mine!"

The Silhouette moved to face Rordyn. She slashed at the clay figure, but the blade bounced off ineffectively. As she brought the blade down a second time, a cold clay hand caught and closed around Rordyn's wrist, and the triumph in her eyes turned to shock and terror, a scream erupting finally as the bones were crushed in the inhuman grip, the useless sword dropping to the ground.

"Fool!" Anyi spat. "You think a wizard's power can so easily be stolen?"

The Silhouette tossed Rordyn aside like a wet kerchief. She hit the base of a tree but managed to roll before the clay hand could catch her again. She scrambled away, plunging down the embankment to the river's edge and splashing into the knee-deep water. The Silhouette stopped at the top of the embankment.

Rordyn laughed again, but this time tinged with hysteria rather than triumph. "It can't; it's clay. No matter what holds it together, it can't follow me. I've won!"

The sound of the shallow fording changed as the Heartstone glowed brighter.

"What are you doing? I can't move my feet. Let go!" Rordyn's panic grew as the water began to rise all around her. Anyi watched, strangely dispassionate, as Rordyn struggled to move feet magically held to the river's bottom. The water swirled and rose until her shouts became gurgling, water-strangled pleas; then silence as the water swirled above her head. When the river subsided, the woman was gone, her body swept downstream.

Anyi'd thought watching Rordyn die would satisfy her, somehow ease her grief. Instead, she felt even more empty and numb than before.

It hadn't brought her beloved Tollan

back.

Nothing would.

"I won't run," she heard Gaelen say. The Silhouette turned to face the lad.

"I deserve to die." Gaelen spoke quietly, his eyes bleak. "I'm sorry, Mistress, I'm so sorry."

"Why?" Anyi managed to ask as her desire for revenge drained away with the lowering waters. "Why did you do this?"

"I didn't know! She said she wanted to talk to Master Tollan. Said she'd been his apprentice before me and she wanted to show what she'd learned since leaving."

"Why didn't you stop her?"

"It happened so fast." Gaelen broke then, falling to his knees. "She told me she wanted to surprise you and Master Tollan. She said she was sure you'd be happy to see her. Called herself your long-lost daughter. She seemed so sincere, and I . . . I believed her. I blocked the wards and let her in. She ran ahead of me while I replaced the wards. By the time I reached the workshop, she'd already bound Master Tollan and pulled out a sword." He paused then, his voice tight with shame. "I froze when

I saw it, Mistress," he said miserably. "A moment, just a moment," a sob shook him, "too long, just a moment and . . . if I'd just done something, said something!" The horror of what he'd witnessed, and failed to prevent, choked him. It was a long time before he could speak again. "And then it was over. Master Tollan was dead, and Rordyn was dragging me out of the house. I'm so sorry." He bowed his head, tears falling freely, the slosh of the river accompanying his sobs.

Anyi watched the wretched young man, son of her house these past four years, and her heart broke again. He, too, was a victim of Rordyn's madness. His apprenticeship, his esteemed teacher, a man he loved the same as a father, even his innocence—all lost in a single stroke.

The first gray light of pre-dawn filled the air. The Silhouette stood motionless beside Anyi, watching in eyeless scrutiny.

Then she felt Tollan's gentle presence again. Like the molding of the Silhouette, a new knowledge bloomed unbidden in her mind. Anyi looked from the Silhouette to the slowly brightening sky, then reached up and unclasped the Heartstone from around the clay neck.

"Gaelen." She said, and he looked up to see her standing over him. "You have much to learn and precious little time." She placed the Heartstone around his neck and saw, in the shock of his widening eyes, the knowledge—and forgiveness—Tollan's ever gentle spirit was imparting.

The sun glinted over the horizon, sending shafts of light toward the three figures. One ray of light touched the clay Silhouette, melting it back into a pile of lifeless clay. Another touched the Heartstone, and a shaft of blue light reflected off it toward Anyi's own heart. She heard Tollan's whispered goodbye and felt the eternity of his love.

As the Heartstone dimmed and went out, Anyi thought the sun seemed to shine more brightly than usual as it climbed into the cloudless sky.

RESEARCH
by
Cat Greenberg

If a story could be described musically as a "little ditty," it would describe this ultra short-short. I would be willing to bet many have suspected this at some time or other. I certainly have!

Xuphxdi phased into the remote lab. Since it was an observation lab, there was a minimal amount of equipment: monitor screen to observe the subject, a console to record reactions, and, of course, the portable dimensional phase shift generator. The cramped space meant they had to shift back home for everything from meals to toilet breaks. Not too long ago, they'd had a lot more room on these missions, but now space was severely limited.

Xuphxdi pulled her lab coat off the circuit board she'd hung it on, quickly wriggling all four tentacles through before extending the claws on her primaries. She slid into the seat beside her mentor.

"How's it going, Dr. Yvqiji?"

"Hello, Xuphxdi. We're very close. Just one more incident, and my theories may well be proven." She smiled; he was positively gleeful.

"Claws crossed," she said. "What's the subject doing?"

"She has spent three of their time units putting code changes into the program," he said, pointing to the human on the screen. The computer whirred all around them.

"Without saving?" she asked hopefully.

"Without saving," he confirmed. "The level of complication in the work seems directly related to their ability to remember such a crucial step. They become too engrossed."

"I think they have singular brains, not divided as ours are. Perhaps one function displaces the other?"

"Interesting hypothesis. You should

talk to the biology department about it."

The communication device sounded, and the human went to it. The screen translated the conversation about deadlines missed and promises that the project would be completed today.

The whirr of the computer surrounding them changed.

"It's happening! This is it!"

The human hung up and returned to the console, muttering about overpaid tech leads wanting a dog and pony show. Her face changed as her attention returned to the computer. Then her face contorted, and the screen had trouble translating what she was saying. Her keystrokes became more and more forceful. Then the subject screamed, momentarily overloading several of their inputs.

"Are you getting all the data?" Xuphxdi asked.

"Yes! Oh, this is wonderful!"

"I don't think she'd agree."

"True," Dr. Yvqiji said, sounding a little regretful. "Sometimes the experiments are uncomfortable for the test subjects. Can't be helped."

The floor suddenly tipped below

them as the CPU was picked up, sending Xuphxdi and Dr. Yvqiji scrambling for sucker and claw holds. Xuphxdi watched in horror as an open window loomed closer on the screen.

"She's berserk! Phase out!"

"Save my data!" shouted Dr. Yvqiji.

"No time, professor!"

Xuphxdi grabbed Dr. Yvqiji with two tentacles, hitting the phase button with a third as the CPU sailed through the air.

Two beings, in different dimensions, simultaneously sighed in resignation and said, "Back to square one."

THE KEEPER OF SOFTER SOULS

by
Cat Greenberg

I am unabashedly an animal lover—if it has fur, I'd probably cuddle it. I've had many wonderful fur children over the years, unique spirits whom I have loved and received love from in return. This story uses many of their names in memory of them, and two who were Bari's, one of whom I had the pleasure to know, as well.

I consider this story to be science fiction. Some may call it fantasy. Perhaps it is somewhere in between.

The squeal of tires jolted Dori from her weeding; a piercing yelp of pain followed. She dropped her trowel and ran for the garage. Throwing up the door, she pulled out her electric tricycle

148

and hitched up the cart she used for the transport of larger dogs for burial. She tossed in leather gloves, a blanket, two large towels, plus the veterinary med kit Peter had "accidentally" left at her house. Then she hopped on the bike and headed down the five-hundred-foot driveway through the two acres of pet cemetery she kept on her property.

Evening was always the worst on this old road. Most of the time she was too late, but occasionally one could be saved. Raphael had been one such. The Russian blue lost half his tail and one leg but got around handily on the other three.

Pulling close to the road, she scanned along it, more than half expecting to see the body of Jake, the careless black lab who lived on the farm west of her place. She finally spied a golden lump half in the ditch a little way down on the other side of the road.

"Oh dear," she said. Not a dog at all, but a coyote.

She walked quietly toward it, seeing the chest rise and fall, ragged and shallow but alive.

"You poor thing," she said softly, trying to sound as non-threatening as possible. She gave him a wide berth at first, surveying the damage. His back legs were twisted unnaturally, and he licked blood coming from his mouth. His eyes watched her, and he whimpered a weak growl, trying to lift his head.

Well, she thought, *I don't think you're a threat.*

Dori walked the trike and cart up behind the coyote and pulled out the kit. She suspected he was at least partly paralyzed, but it might be shock, and shock wears off. She took out a syringe and a vial of acepromazine, a sedative and muscle relaxer. As a retired vet tech, she was a pretty good judge of weight and measured out the dose she thought would be right.

"I'm going to hope really hard, pretty baby, that you understand I'm trying to help." *Please, Lord, tell him I'm here to help.*

She talked soothingly, moving with slow, fluid motions. Urgent as his injuries clearly were, sudden movement would panic him and make things worse. She knelt down near his head, and still he didn't move, only whined and watched her with fiercely frightened eyes.

She ventured her gloved left hand slowly toward his nose, coming from below his chin. The nose wriggled, sniffing. She continued to talk softly, keeping his attention while her right hand brought the needle down into his shoulder. The coyote was so weak that he barely flinched; then he visibly relaxed as the drug took effect.

"There," she said, only now venturing to stroke his golden throat. His eyes were glazing over. She got out the blanket and spread it on the ground behind him. She lifted his back legs and cringed—the bones felt shattered. She then got his shoulders on the blanket and slid him into the cart, securing the back and collecting up her kit. As she turned back onto the driveway, she pulled out her cell phone.

"Pete? I've got an injured coyote. Hurry Pete,it's bad."

Peter's house and clinic were a mile up the road. Would he be fast enough?

An hour later the coyote was lying on Dori's kitchen table with an IV hooked up to him.

"I'm sorry, Dori. There's nothing I can do but make him comfortable. His hips are shattered, as you suspected, and I think the base of his spine is severed. Can't be certain without an X-ray, but," he shook his head sadly, "there's just too much damage."

Dori sat by the coyote's head, stroking his beautiful ears and soft rough. His eyes came in and out of focus as pain killer continued to drip into his leg vein.

"Poor little lad," she said.

"I am amazed, really, that he's lasted this long. I could give him something stronger, make it quick."

"No. He's out of pain, let it come naturally."

"All right. While I'm here, I think I'll make the rounds of your menagerie."

Dori smiled slightly, knowing it was an excuse to give her privacy as the coyote passed.

The coyote's eyes cleared again and looked into Dori's. He accepted that he was dying. Dori did not think animals feared death like humans, having no concept of intangible reasoning such as why? And what's next? To them, death is just a natural course. What animals fear are the tangible things, like threat and pain. The coyote understood that Dori took the pain away. He understood that she was not a threat. There was no fear in those clear, gold eyes as she stroked him, her voice a gentle, soothing timbre.

His breath grew more shallow as she felt the others arrive. First came Fidget, never far from her mind. He was their first puppy, a Border Collie-Shepard mix who fell victim to lymphoma. Then came Cassie and Ty, her Samoyeds, rescued from a puppy mill, who'd died young from congenital heart defects. Then Sharra and Houdini, cats who'd lived to ripe old ages.

It wasn't like movies or books where anthropomorphized animals speak English into the minds of their companions. Dori felt their presence in her mind in very animal ways. The sound of a purr only she could hear, the feel of a tail wagging in joy, or the peaceful quiet that was a rabbit's occasional snuggle of contentment in the corner of her awareness. Many were brief visits, like from those who rested in the cemetery, but the ones most beloved by her and her late husband, Jeremy, never completely left her.

"It's all right," she told the coyote. "You have friends here."

She felt the release as the body stilled and heard the howl in her mind. It was joyous, the sound of exuberant freedom. It swirled and wrapped around her, an embrace of gratitude. The others greeted the newcomer in celebration, then their presence faded, leaving only the afterglow when Peter came back.

"He's gone?"

She nodded and smiled, tearing up a little. "Although I think he may stay awhile."

Peter shook his head. He always walked the fence with regard to Dori's "gift." He admitted he'd seen some strange things; still she knew he couldn't quite convince himself, man of science that he was, to believe in Dori's ghostly fur friends. But after fifty years of friendship, it was enough for him that *she* believed.

Dori took a portable flood lamp off the wall as Peter gently wrapped the coyote to carry it to the pet cemetery. After they were finished putting dirt over the new grave, they walked in companionable silence back to the house.

"How about a cup of tea?" she asked as they reached the porch. "I have Darjeeling."

"Definitely," he agreed. "But before I forget, you should bring Prince in for a blood test. It's time to check the thyroid dose again."

"I'll call Jenny for an appointment," she said, filling the kettle with water. "Everyone else okay?"

"Everyone I could *find*. Jazzy eluded me."

Jazzy usually did. As a tiny stray kitten, the little tortie cat had had a house demolished around her and still startled and ran at the slightest noise—especially Peter trying to find her for a check-up.

They had tea on the back deck. From her hilltop home, Dori had a spectacular view of the Ozarks. On really clear days, she could just make out the glint of lake water ten miles away. The stars were bright over the valley below with thin, scattered clouds helping the full moon's glow to cast everything in a fairy twilight.

"Will you look at that?" Peter said, suddenly standing up and walking to the far railing. Dori joined him, and he pointed at the stars over the valley.

Three reddish lights were moving in a slow triangle low in the sky. They watched as one seemed to drop toward the valley, skimming the tops of the trees five miles or so away. After a few minutes, it rejoined the other two. Then the triangle stopped, hovering in place.

"Helicopters?" Dori asked. Military helicopters were not an unusual sight.

"Could be, but they wouldn't be red. You'd think we'd be able to hear helicopters."

Dori listened, but the only sound was the orchestrated chirp and whistle of insects punctuated by a few night birds. A slight breeze blew in the direction of the lights, but not enough to push sound away.

"They may be farther away than they look," Dori said.

Then with mouth-dropping suddenness the lights zipped off in separate directions. In a blink, they were gone.

"That was interesting," said Dori, "I've never seen a helicopter do that."

"No," Peter scowled, "but lasers could. There're just enough clouds for some of the bigger toys you can buy now. The army base has been having a lot of trouble lately with people pointing them at helicopter cockpits and bouncing them off unregistered drones."

"Those pranks are going to make someone crash one of these days," Dori said, shaking her head at the stupidity of fools.

An hour of pleasant conversation later, and Dori was walking Peter to his truck.

"Thanks for coming and helping with the coyote."

"Anytime, dear lady." He took her hand, bowed over it, and kissed it. "I am at your beck and call."

Dori watched Peter pull onto the road, still smiling as she turned back toward the house. She knew he was hoping for more than friendship someday. His wife had passed a year before Jeremy, and Peter often expressed his feelings of loneliness. She did care deeply for him, and they had much in common. Maybe someday she would be ready to encourage his hope.

The husky she'd taken in when he was a year old came up beside her, butting her hand with his head.

"Time for bed, Teddi?" she asked, rubbing his head absently and scratching behind his ears. She yawned. "Definitely."

Except for the terrible ache of missing Jeremy, Dori didn't mind living alone. She never worried about security, since her "menagerie" included Teddi, plus Eveshka, a Shepard-Great Pyrenees mix who got her size from the Pyrenees parent (but thankfully with less slobber), and Rom, a fluffy, scared-of-everything jumble of breeds who was a louder burglar alarm than anything with wires. Dori had even made a little sign for her yard. It read:

MY BURGLAR ALARM HAS TEETH
AND FINDS YOU TASTY.

For more companionship she had her indoor cats, Jazzy, Prince, and

158

Jerimiah, and the barn cats, Little Bit, Harry, Porthos, and of course, Raphael, who had decided he preferred life outside to life inside. So Dori slept secure and with plenty of company on the king-size bed.

Dori flipped the covers back and got stiffly out of bed, like a toy manipulated by a child. Jazzy, Prince, and Rom, who'd all been asleep on the bed with her, were frozen motionless, their eyes wide with fear. Inside her mind, a cold, antiseptic presence was growing. She tried to scream, but nothing came out. Was she awake? Was she dreaming?

She reached the front door, turned the dead bolt, and stepped barefoot onto the porch. Something sat at the bottom of her driveway near the road. It glowed softly like a large ruby, and there was an odd shape moving in front of it. She stepped off the porch and into the grass, walking down the long hill toward the glow.

Whatever that was at the bottom of the hill, it was the source of the presence in her head. All the science fiction stories she'd ever read sprang to life.

This was not a human, and it might not see Dori as anything but a specimen. She tried and failed to block the control it exerted, becoming more frightened with each step forward.

The feeling inside her mind changed as the presence began to sift through her memories. Tears streamed down her face as she saw her parents again, her sister, friends long gone, reliving events as vividly as if they were happening now. Every joy and every sorrow. It seemed especially interested in feelings of sorrow and loss; they were intoxicating to it, and she could feel how foreign and enticing the sensation was.

It was a violation. That thing had no right to her memories!

She saw her beloved Jeremy, lying in the hospital bed, tubes coming out of every part of him.

Her mind screamed. *No! Not Jeremy! You cannot have him!*

The memory image blurred, the sound of a purr replacing the beeping of medical devices.

The bark of a dog joined the purr, and Dori pushed back with every ounce of will she could muster.

"Get out!" Her scream rang through the silence as she stopped among the headstones.

Her voice!

The clammy presence of the alien mind was losing its grip. Another presence was pushing through. Several others. Fidget put himself between her mind and that of the alien, barking. The gentle purr became a roar filling her, pushing the wedge larger. The alien mind reeled at the presence of the animal spirits, failing to exert control over them. Ty and Cassie showed up as fierce growling, but still the alien pushed back. Dori couldn't make herself retreat to the house, but they'd managed to interrupt her progress down the hill.

The siege went on for an eternity, hot knives piercing Dori's head in a tug and pull battle for her mind. Her vision was red fog. How long could they keep up this struggle for her will?

The bright, wild howl of the coyote shot through, a vivid burst of gold following the telepathic link to its alien source. The alien mind staggered at the impact of the attack and fled her mind. The control severed, Dori collapsed.

Arms caught her. Dazed, she realized it was Peter. Eveshka and Teddi were with him as Rom and the cats, freed of the immobilizing control, came racing out of the house, joined by the barn cats. All headed down the hill toward the alien.

"How? How did you know?" She managed to ask.

"Teddi and 'Veshka came to my house," he said panting. "I knew something was wrong, but I couldn't," he had to pause for breath, "my car died halfway here. We ran the rest of the way." She remembered Teddi and Eveshka uncharacteristically hadn't wanted to come in with Rom. It was a nice night, so she'd left them loose outside.

Dori and Peter moved to huddle by the dogwoods and watch as the odd-looking alien, what they could see of it, backed away from three barking, growling dogs and seven hissing and spitting cats. Dori could sense it trying in vain to immobilize her defenders, but it could not penetrate the spirit animals' protective shield. She could feel the coyote's fierce attack continuing, nipping at the creature's mind, then flitting away only to come back from another direction. The alien recoiled and retreated into its ship. In a flair of light, it was gone.

For a long while, she and Peter just sat there, holding on to each other, and then to the dogs, as all three joined them, licking faces and wagging tails. The cats paced and prowled, circling them, Jazzy climbing into Peter's lap, of all things.

"Are you all right, Dori?" Peter asked, finally breaking the silence.

Dori took a deep breath, nodding. "I think so. The outcome could have been much worse."

Peter chuckled. "My dear, ever practical, lady." He hugged her, quiet again, then said, "It was like you were a walking statue, Dori. I tried, but I couldn't pull you away." Dori looked at the shock and amazement in his eyes. "Then you screamed and stopped, but I still couldn't budge you. Your eyes were open, but I don't think you could see me."

She shook her head. "I had no idea you were there, and I couldn't control my body. It made me relive old memories, painful ones. It tried to make me relive Jeremy's death. My emotions were like a drug, getting it high."

"Dori," he began as though unsure how to tell her something, "when you screamed, I saw, I mean—I couldn't have seen—but I did." She tilted her head in puzzlement at his rambling. "I would swear I saw Fidget standing in front of you, and Ty and Cassie on either side, and Sharra and Houdini on either shoulder. It's impossible, but . . . "

"You did," she interrupted him, "you did." She put her hand on his. "They broke through the alien's hold on me. Maybe what the aliens were doing made them visible to you. Or you're more sensitive than you think."

He looked down a minute, then back at her.

"I saw a streak of gold shoot out of your eyes, Dori." He sounded like he desperately wanted her to tell him it hadn't happened, but she only smiled.

"The coyote," she said. "He attacked it. I think he's still with whoever that being was." Then she tilted her head thoughtfully. "I wonder if aliens believe in ghosts."

"Do you think it'll be back? Bring its friends?"

"Not if they know what's good for them," she said as they stood up. Dori stretched and brushed off her pajamas. The sky was the gray of predawn with a rim of orange promising a beautiful sunrise.

An old pick-up truck drove by, and the morning paper was thrown onto the driveway. Amazingly normal, like any other day. Peter retrieved it, bringing it back, laughing as he looked at the front page.

He held it up to show Dori.

ARMY DENIES LIGHTS ARE UFO'S

"Think we should correct them?" he asked. She rolled her eyes and shook her head.

"And become a cable television special? No thanks. Who cares what they believe? What I think," she continued, putting her arm through Peter's, "is that we should have breakfast."

SACRIFICE AND SOLACE

by
Cat Greenberg

The germ of this story came during an old television episode about a poltergeist. (Kind of funny since the story doesn't even have a ghost in it.) So I jotted down the "hmm, what if . . .?" and stashed it away. It took a long while for it to percolate in my brain's alluvial sludge and become a story.

Queen Joia listened for the cry of life from her firstborn. None came. She closed her eyes and prayed for the magic of her lineage to continue. So much depended on this birth.

"Well?" she called to the midwife, unable to wait any longer. Finally the words she'd been waiting for flooded her with relief.

"Vyrlin is stillborn, Majesty," the midwife said in triumph.

"The Mother be praised," Queen Joia whispered, tears spilling as she reached to bless her child. "Go in peace to the netherplane, my daughter, and grow in power, to fulfill the Mother's will."

Pain returned, throwing her back on the cushions. The midwife carefully bundled the tiny body then handed the older twin to the Servant of the Mother before turning her attention back to the younger twin's demands.

Joia had no time to help push this child out; her body took over, convulsing her with a scream as her heir found the world. A sharp, piercing wail left no room to doubt her arrival.

"Young Vyrdis already shows her strength." said the midwife.

"Good," Joia whispered, exhaustion vying with elation as the babe was cleaned and brought to her. "You will need it, my daughter. I pray the battle does not come before you are ready.

Vyrdis lifted her head from the table where she'd nodded off trying to memorize crystal variations. Opening her eyes, she froze.

A moonless, starless night would have been brighter. More than the absence of light, it was the devouring of it. She reached for the lamp on the table where she'd nodded off, feeling the heat. It still burned, the glow completely swallowed.

The Darkening.

Tygax.

She closed her eyes again and quickly bound them with the sash from around her waist. Open eyes would attract the demon's attention, like a dog who can smell the treat in your pocket. Through open eyes, the Darkening could draw out the Blessed Mother's Light, along with your soul for the demon to feed on. Now it was up to Vyrlin to grant what sight Vyrdis needed.

Vyrdis relaxed and reached, sending her mind to the netherplane, her spirit-self raising palms to her twin sister. Vyrlin was Vyrdis's mirror image here; were they both mortal, no one would have been able to tell them apart. However, Vyrlin was spirit-born; she'd never touched the earth within a mortal body, her stillborn shell abandoned as she left their earth-mother's womb. The rarest form of Yldinin magic was more powerful than a mortal body could survive, so it passed to the elder twin, who held it on the netherplane. The ability to wield this magic passed to the younger twin, who depended upon the elder for the wisdom and detachment of never having been mortal.

"Tygax is freed; the Darkening has come," Vyrdis said.

A thousand years ago, the Yldin mages had only managed to imprison the demon. But a prophecy told of the unprecedented birth of two linked generations of mage twins, the Blessed Mother's Chosen, heralding the weakening of the bonds holding Tygax, when the Yldin would again battle the demon. Vyrdis and Vyrlin were the second generation, their mother, Queen Joia, with her twin, Joicina, were the first.

"They say we may not survive the Joining." It was the first time Vyrdis admitted her fear, but Vyrlin only nodded.

"Much power will flow, but do not allow your faith to be shaken, Vyrdis. Even if we perish, it is a small price to pay for the fate of our people."

Vyrdis took a deep breath and nodded. "The Joining of five could only imprison him. I only hope eight is enough to destroy him."

"Even if he is simply imprisoned again, it is better than leaving him loose. We can only pray for the strength to fight, then trust in Our Blessed Mother's Light."

Vyrdis laid her crossed palms over her heart, mirror of her sister. "Great Mother, give us strength," they prayed in unison

The Light of the Mother filled Vyrdis with peace and clarity. They were not alone in their fight. When she opened her eyes, the resolve she felt was reflected in the glow of her sister's spirit-eyes.

"It is time," Vyrlin said. Vyrdis left the netherplane and returned to her body.

The comfort and strength of her spirit-twin touched her mind. She carefully blew out the lamp and headed for the door. The Chronicles told of the first Darkening when many burned alive in fire they could not see to escape. She felt Vyrlin's guidance in her mind as she made her way across the room. The others would be heading for Blessing Hill in the same manner, while the people followed the guide stones set throughout the city, leading them to gather with the Servants of the Mother in the wide courtyards of the four commons.

Vyrdis took a deep breath of the cool night air as she opened her door. Was there a hint of smoke already? She descended the steps of the house on the edge of the city, where she'd spent her year of living with the Crafters. As heir she was required to live one year with each caste to understand the people she would rule. Unfortunately, this year it put her a fair distance from Blessing Hill.

As she walked down the street, there was an eerie quiet. The usual din of anvil, chisel, and hammer was silenced.

Silence is good, she thought and hoped she would continue to hear nothing. The people had been warned and drilled on what to do, wearing sashes like hers at all times to be able to quickly bind their eyes. She imagined an orderly procession of joined hands, heading to the commons. Vyrdis judged herself halfway to Craft Masters Street when she began to feel the heat of buildings afire. The speed with which the disaster manifested shocked her. Then she began to hear the sounds she dreaded: shouts, crying, and screams. Panic was as much their enemy as the demon itself.

Yes, sadly many are panicking, sister, but more are following the instructions, came Vyrlin's reassurance.

As she felt the paving stones change to the smoother glass of Artisan Square, the acrid stench of burnt flesh stung her. She pulled the edge of the sash over her nose, wishing she'd doused the sash with water before leaving. It was worse than when the Plague at Byentin wiped out half the town two winters ago. The bodies they'd burned then were already dead; these she feared were not.

"Great Mother, help me!" a man pleaded, running into her and grabbing at her arms. It took a moment for her to recognize the voice of Stonemaster Jardin.

Before she could say anything, a scream she would never have thought human tore violently from his throat, and he fell against her feet. Vyrlin deftly guided her around his prone form. Vyrdis stopped, filled with guilt and grief. Jardin was a good man, with a wife, children, how could he be lost this way? She should do something. A vile gurgling filled the air, and Vyrdis choked. She covered her ears, desperate to block out the sound of the Demon gorging on the light of the man's forfeited soul.

Move! Vyrlin's painfully sharp command in her mind startled Vyrdis into walking again. Another scream, a woman, not far ahead.

There is no helping them here, sister mine, Vyrlin reminded her firmly. *He wants you to delay and falter. He will do everything he can to distract and mislead you.*

"I should help them," Vyrdis whispered.

You are helping them. They were warned about the Darkening and instructed on what to do when it came. Hundreds are gathering, eyes bound, holding to one another, guided by the Servants in prayer and trusting the Chosen to stop Tygax. The ones who panic are lost, Vyrdis; there is nothing you can do for them.

Vyrdis locked her jaw on her stomach's threatened rebellion and pictured her cousin, Jerim, sitting blindfolded, holding to his wife, Julena, and little Dani, who would be six next month. Yes. She could anchor herself with the thought of their safety. They would be in Talimin Commons, surrounded by the faithful, waiting for the Mother's Chosen to save them. Depending on them; depending on her.

She focused on the simple act of dragging one foot in front of the other.

Left.

Then right.

Just one step at a time.

Gradually the sounds of terror diminished as her concentration tightened and the world shrank to the motion of walking.

Left.

Nothing else mattered. All sense of time and direction was lost.

Right.

Only the motion of her legs. Trust Vyrlin to take care of her course.

Left.

She barely noticed the paving stone turn to dirt as she passed the edge of the city. Not until she felt the resistance of climbing the slope of Blessing Hill did she allow her focus to lessen to keep from falling.

As she reached the top of Blessing Hill, the wind was whipping into a gale, and the sensation of lightning sparked through the air and prickled her skin. Unlike a natural storm, no thunder followed, just the roar of wind. She reached as she came to the crest, wondering if the others had arrived or if she was alone with only her spirit-sister to face Tygax.

We are not alone, Vyrlin assured as she guided Vyrdis to the four waiting clerics, solo mages who would add their power and act as conduits, linking the two pairs of twin magic together.

"Where is my mother?" Vyrdis called out, her throat tightened at the Queen's absence.

A cleric tried to answer, but the words were lost in the storm and the groan and crash of collapsing buildings coming from the city below.

She is near, Vyrlin assured her. *I can feel Joicina.* The wait stretched on interminably to Vyrdis.

"I am here," came Queen Joia's voice, and Vyrdis's heart leapt to her throat. A familiar hand touched her shoulder, and she whirled to fiercely embrace her earth-mother.

"It is worse than I ever imagined," she said, near to tears at the relief of her mother's arrival. "Will we be enough?"

"The trouble with prophecies," Queen Joia said in her daughter's ear, "is they only guide you *to* the battle; they never tell you who will win." Then she took her daughter's face in her hands. "But *I* am telling you—we *will* succeed."

Vyrdis nodded, resolved to match her mother's grim determination. They moved into position and removed their blindfolds. The greatest peril came now, since they must open their eyes at the precise moment when the Joining completed, not before, or the demon would consume their souls, the circle broken.

Vydis saw in her mind's eye her mother, standing opposite her on the summit, hands outstretched to either side as she began the Joining ritual, Joicina behind Joia as Vyrlin stood behind Vyrdis. Two clerics each stood to her left and right, ready to be links in the chain, completing the gestalt.

"As it was foretold a thousand years past, the Joyful Harbinger of Our Blessed Mother's Light," this was the meaning of the Queen's twin names, "will become one with the Vanquisher of Evil's Darkness," the meaning of Vyrdis's twin names. "We Join ourselves in the Name and Light of Our Blessed Mother."

Vyrdis felt the tingle of power build all around her, pushing against the Darkening as the first two clerics clasped wrists with the Queen. Stinging dust pelted her face and arms. Vyrdis staggered as a tree branch crashed into her calves. Grunts and cries around her told how the others were being similarly battered.

A woman's cry, a familiar voice, erupted from behind where Queen Joia stood.

"Dani!"

Vyrdis was stunned. They should be safely at the commons. They'd rehearsed it a hundred times. Why was she here?

Because I brought her here, a voice oozed in her mind.

Vyrdis's stomach tightened.

"Jerim?" Vyrdis called.

He has been . . . detained. The voice was a growling snake, slinking through an oily pool. *I trust he can swim?*

"Dani, where are you?" The cry was desperate.

"Mama!" Little Dani's terror hung in the air.

"No, Julena! Don't!"

But Vyrdis was too late, and her cries became the tortured shriek of the demon feasting on Julena's soul.

"Our Mother's Light will defeat the dark," the Queen intoned, her voice strained and raspy as the second pair of clerics clasped wrists with the first pair. The air crackled with power.

"Through the Vanquisher of Evil's Darkness, whose sword is the Blessed Mother's Light." Vyrdis felt the cleric's hands reaching toward hers.

"Go 'way!" Came Dani's petrified wailing.

Finish and she dies, the demon hissed in her mind, and Vyrdis's hands stopped before they touched the cleric's.

The whisper of the demon slithered through her, feeding the seed of her earlier guilt. Then Vyrlin's presence glowed brighter, driving Tygax's intrusion back.

"I'm sorry, Dani, I can't.," Vyrdis whispered, trying to steel her resolve, "he'll destroy everyone."

And how many will your circle destroy? Tygax pushed back harder. *Your mother? The whole city? Do you even know?*

Could it be that many? Was there any choice?

Perhaps I will be reasonable. Its tone turned seductive. *Perhaps you can offer me something to save them. Something—unique—something born once in a thousand years.*

179

Her sense of balance failed, and her half-raised hands fell limp.

"You want me." A flat statement.

Yes, Heirling, it hissed, *sacrifice yourself, not your mother. This child. Let go the circle!*

"Vyrdis!" Joia fought to speak through the unfinished gestalt. "The circle must be completed!"

Tears welled up under her closed eyelids, spilling down her face as she slowly reached her hands toward the clerics. Dani's voice changed pitch then, turning wild, and Vyrdis's hands stopped short again.

It is you who cause the child pain, Heirling! Even if you destroy me, I will kill her first. Will you sacrifice one so young? Open your eyes! I will take the Yldinin Heir instead. It hissed in her mind. *You will be her savior, instead of her executioner.*

"I can't," she whispered, and Dani screamed.

"Wait! If I give you my soul, will you leave this place forever?"

Forever? There was a rumbling in her mind. *A long time forever, even for me.*

"Will you do it?" She pressed.

For the Soul of the Yldinin Heir?

Vyrdis let her tightly shut eyelids relax.

It is easy to sacrifice yourself, sister mine, Vyrlin's voice pushed past the voice of the demon. *Harder to sacrifice another, even when it is the right choice. You must complete the Joining.*

"Vyrdis, please," her mother pleaded. "Don't trust . . ."

"I will make my own choice!" Vyrdis hissed and felt the demon's pleasure and anticipation.

Yes. Yes. Your soul, and I will leave, forever, as you say. His grotesque anticipation was palpable.

"Release the child, as a show of faith. Proof you will hold to your bargain," Vyrdis told it.

Tygax considered her request, distracted in its eagerness. As it turned its attention from Vyrdis to Dani, Vyrdis's hands flew up to grasp the wrists of the second two clerics.

No! Tygax shrieked in her mind. *Trickster!*

Vyrdis gasped as the fire of magic filled her, bliss and torment blending as one. Every breath was a struggle, and her knees threatened to give way.

In unison the circle of mages opened their eyes, and Vyrdis groaned, drenched in the liquid flame of the combined magic. Radiance poured from their eyes, pooled in the center of the circle, swirling, growing, then shot out of the circle, the blades of a thousand avenging swords slicing through the Darkening.

The unnatural dark lifted, and the brilliance coalesced back within the circle, power building further. The hideous shape of the demon emerged. More shadow than substance, it crept around the circle, sometimes upright and sometimes crawling, dragging Dani by one leg. The empty shell of Julena lay crushed beneath its pacing. Vyrdis's heart raced when she saw Dani's arms were flung tightly over her eyes. She was not yet lost!

Vyrdis looked around the circle. All showed the same barely contained agony Vyrdis felt, and all the knowledge of what must be done. Which of these lives must she burn out to rid their land of this evil? Or would The Blessed Mother take them all?

Sister, help me!

You can do this, came Vyrlin's calm encouragement. *The power builds. If it chooses to take one of us, or all of us, so be it. They accept the choice. For Tygax to be destroyed, so also must you.*

It was for Vyrdis and Vyrlin, so named Vanquisher, to pull on the strength of the gestalt and focus the fullness of the power in a final sword thrust at Tygax. Vyrdis sent as much love through the link as she could, part apology for what she must do and part admiration and gratitude for the gift they were willing to give. She felt the same returned to her and nodded.

"Now, sister mine," she said.

Vyrlin pulled the full power of the Joining to her on the netherplane and wove it together to send to Vyrdis.

A snarling roar from the demon as it stalked around the circle was all the warning given before it slammed into Joia's back, knocking her to her knees. The glowing form of Joicina could be seen now that the gestalt was complete, but the demon's claws raked impotently through her. The demon raged, turning its attention to the cleric on the Queen's right. Claws found purchase in skin, and the cleric fell forward, straining to keep hold as blood poured from the slashes on his shoulder. One by one, Tygax attacked the clerics, trying to physically break the circle.

Angry tears drying in the wind, Vyrdis accepted the power from Vyrlin and turned her gaze on the shadowy form as it poised to strike the next cleric.

A shrill, monstrous keening filled the air as Vyrdis sent the full force of the power out. Drenched in the Mother's Light, the demon's agony echoed and reverberated in Her retribution. There were strangled cries from the clerics as the magic's price was paid. Joia screamed, and the image of Joicina faltered.

Dani was flung aside as the glow increased, enveloping the demon before slowly rising into the night sky like a new sun. High above them, the glow burst into a blinding shower of stars.

As the radiance faded, the gestalt suddenly released. Silence howled in Vyrdis's ears as she sank to her knees and saw the lifeless eyes of the clerics' charred bodies staring into the night sky. Vyrdis crawled to where her mother lay limp in the grass, barely breathing.

"I told you," she struggled to whisper as Vyrdis gathered her into her arms, "we would succeed."

Her mother managed to reach a hand up to touch her daughter's cheek in a last caress, brushing away tears.

"Take care. . . of our people," she said, a final sigh as Vyrdis held her close and wept.

Tygax was destroyed, their people safe, but the price was so high. Vyrlin was right, it would have been easier to sacrifice herself. What comfort could she offer those who remained when she could not even console herself?

A muffled whimper reached her ears, and she looked up. Dani sat clutching her knees, her head on her small arms. Vyrdis gently laid her mother down, crossing her palms in final prayer over her mother's lifeless heart, then kissing her forehead. She struggled to pull herself up, scrubbed the tears from her face, and staggered over to the child, picking her up. She checked to see if

Dani was badly hurt. Cuts and bruises, no more.

"Shh," she soothed. "The nightmare is over." It was only then that Dani's tears fell in earnest.

The sky began to lighten with the promise of dawn as Vyrdis looked over to where the clerics and her mother lay, then down at the ruins of the city. Straggles of people were falteringly making their way toward the base of the hill.

The wounds of this night went deeper than those still seeping blood and would be slower to mend. In time, perhaps, the safety of this child and those like her would be solace enough. For now, she would do as her mother wished and take care of her people.

The Female of the Species

by

Cat Greenberg

This is the second of the two reprint stories originally published in Marion Zimmer Bradley's Fantasy Magazine *under my previous name. This one actually predates "Lessons in the Dark," as it appeared in Issue 9 in the summer of 1990. The challenge of the issue was all the stories were to be 1,000 words, or less, called a short-short. Not the easiest thing to do.*

With a nod to Rudyard Kipling.

The band of men descended on the quiet settlement like a desert storm—sudden and devastating. Their fierce battle cries thundered through the cool morning air, shattering its illusion of peace. The bandits met no resistance, not even a guard. They dismounted, weapons in hand, and scattered to invade and ransack the tents.

Hakeim, the bandit leader, headed for the large center tent, which was used as court. He entered cautiously, sword raised, until he saw the tent's inhabitants. Several dozen women huddled together in fear in its center. He smiled in lustful appreciation of the selection. His men would praise him tonight indeed!

His lieutenant entered a moment later. "Sir, the settlement is abandoned. No one save these," he indicated the women. "We've met no resistance. Apparently, many items are missing. We will still do well here, but not as well, I suspect, as we could have."

Hakeim dismissed the lieutenant. "Where is your king? Your warriors?" he demanded. "Not even an *old* man is to be found?"

A strikingly beautiful and bejeweled woman in flowing crimson silk walked steadily to the center of the tent. She met hard brown eyes with soft green ones before kneeling. She covered her face with her hands, bowing to the floor in obeisance, her waterfall of black hair spilling coolly over his sandaled feet. After a moment she came up to sit on her heels, hands on her knees and eyes lowered.

"They are gone, my lord. They saw your band coming. Knowing the fearsome reputation of the Great Bandit Hakeim Labahn, they took themselves away with whatever they could carry. I am Talina, Queen of the Natani Tribe. I and my women were left here as a gift to appease you that you might choose not to follow the rest of the tribe. We beg only kind treatment from your noble band," she raised her eyes to meet his with a decidedly sensual eloquence. "Natani women know many ways to please men."

Hakeim felt unbidden heat rise within him. All the desert knew the reputation of the women of Natani, just as all knew *his* reputation for ruthlessness.

He had heard also the cowardly reputation of Natani men. Her story was not implausible. Evidence held to it, even that his far riders had seen a large band leave the settlement yesterday. It was one of the reasons he'd attacked when he did—less resistance; but *no* resistance?

"As Queen," she continued, her searching gaze boring relentlessly into him, "may I exercise my right to choose the Great Bandit Leader for myself?" His leering smile was answer enough.

"I have thirty men who will be very pleased by your offer," he put out a hand to help her rise. "After I have weighed your worth, we will discuss terms to keep your tribe free."

"My women number thirty-six," she purred. "Some of your men will be doubly grateful. Choose carefully those with the stamina for such a gift."

As night fell, the tents were filled again, with bandits led by the women of their choice. Talina took Hakeim into her own bedchamber. He pulled her roughly to him and kissed her soundly, a kiss she returned with passion while her hands suggestively caressed his neck and back. Then she pulled away.

"Would you have me so quickly when I can make your pleasure last for hours?" she asked enticingly.

Her cool, smooth voice spoke volumes to the enthralled bandit leader. She started to undress him, slowly and with great deliberation, then paused at his sword belt.

He removed it for her, then ran his hand over her shoulder, pulling down the silk to reveal her breast. She moved deftly away, giving him her most seductive look yet.

"In time," she smiled and drew him to lie within the nest of cushions that made her bed.

Never had he felt such ecstasy as her ministrations brought. Groaning with pleasure, he closed his eyes, not seeing her hand reach beneath the crimson silk. Then his eyes popped open as the gentle caress became a painful vice grip, and he felt cold, sharp steel press against the all too tender flesh of his manhood. The slightest movement, and he would be a eunuch.

"I trust you're not foolish enough to cry out." The silken voice was now hard ice.

He gaped at her, fighting his sudden and total terror of what she might do. She smiled.

"I wonder how many of your victims have felt the same helpless fear as you raped their women and stole their children to slavery," she mused. "Now the conqueror becomes the captive."

A few moments later the drapes parted, and two women entered, blue and violet silks spattered with blood, which was clearly not their own. He noticed that the one in blue carried his lieutenant's blade. They strode purposefully to the side of the bed, the violet one picking up Hakeim's sword. Drawing it from the scabbard, she placed the tip to his throat. Only then did Talina release his hostaged manhood.

The one in blue bowed slightly.

"The rest of his men are dispatched, my Queen. As you thought, they became complacent in their eagerness to bed us."

Talina nodded.

"Good. The bodies can be piled on the west ridge and burned at sunrise when the winds will carry away the stench. That will signal the tribe it is safe to return."

Hakeim sputtered incoherently. "You *planned* this?" He finally blurted out.

"But of course," Talina responded.

"Your men have no honor!" he spat, "they let their women do their fighting for them!"

Talina chuckled at his pathetic attempt to insult her.

"We are a practical people, Lord Bandit. Had our warriors engaged you head on, lives might have been lost. We found it unacceptable that even a little Natani blood might be spilled over such a worthless rabble. This way, our only loss is a few blood-soiled linens. Your reputation *did* precede you, and your weaknesses were obvious. Does not a good warrior sensibly use his enemy's weakness against him? I see no dishonor in being sensible." She turned to the one in blue.

"Take him into the courtyard," she instructed. "Better yet, walk him to the west ridge, then we won't have to carry his body."

As they left, Talina considered the brigand's utter shock. She thought everyone knew: as with most species, the female human is far deadlier than the male.

EVERY MOTHER'S WISH

by
Cat Greenberg

As the mother of three children, I know this wish has been mine on numerous occasions. I don't think there is a mother out there who hasn't wished for it at least once.

A terrible screech erupted from the depths of the catacombs of the dead. Screams and shouts followed along with crazed laughter. The face of the woman standing near the entrance paled, each voice familiar. Her white-knuckled grip held the harness of the donkey cart, her toddler asleep inside. Her baby squirmed in her other arm. She closed her eyes briefly, gathering herself before adding her own voice to the din.

"Kiril, Lysandra, and Vasos, you get out of there this *instant*!"

The silence was sudden and complete. Three children—ten, nine, and seven, respectively—trudged up the steps one at a time to stand before their exasperated mother.

"How many times have I told you the catacombs are not a playground? The dead have earned their rest and do not need it disturbed by you lot racing around and doing your best to wake them!"

"But Kiril dared me," Lysa protested.

"I don't care if the Holy See of Constantinople dares you. *I* said stay out!"

Three sets of feet shuffled in the dirt, and a contrite "Yes, Mama" was said by all.

"Home," she ordered, "now."

As her errant older offspring departed, Sophronia sighed and shifted Rezi on her hip. The baby had fallen asleep in spite of the exchange, and Sophronia silently thanked Saint Nicholas as she placed Rezi next to Iason. A few moments of peace and free hands to draw water.

"Come on, Luki," she clucked at the donkey, glad he was a fairly placid creature. She guided the cart with a practiced care toward the well.

Sophronia watched the ground as she walked, taking care to avoid rocks and holes that could jar the cart and wake the children. She had just turned the corner toward the square surrounding the village well, blessedly empty at this hour of the day, when she saw the silver glint of a coin in the dirt. Maybe she would have a little luck today after all. She picked it up, disappointed that it was just a faceless disc, not a drachma. She wondered if it was even silver.

Oh well, I should probably check, she thought and started to put it in her pocket.

"Aren't you going to make a wish?"

Sophronia about jumped out her skin at the woman's voice, and even Luki tossed his head.

"Easy," she soothed the donkey, then she turned. "You shouldn't sneak up on people!" It was a harsh whisper. She was angry but would not risk waking the children.

The woman smiled, deep amethyst eyes seeming to draw Sophronia in. "My apologies," she bowed. "The coin," she had a quietly musical voice. "It is a wishing coin. You should make a wish and toss it in the well."

Sophronia looked down at the coin in her calloused hand, then raised an eyebrow to the woman as the coin went purposefully into her pocket.

"Wishing coin?" She laughed, eyeing the woman up and down. "I'll give you credit for dressing the part. A djinn, right? Well you can go scam someone else. I don't have time for this. I need to get water."

Sophronia pulled her cart past the woman.

"But you could wish never to need to get water again. Or wish for gold to hire someone else to get it for you."

Sophronia stopped and turned, annoyed that the woman wouldn't take no for an answer.

"And be drowned in a flood? Or buried alive in coins? Or maybe have a murderous thief come after my family to return his ill-gotten gains?"

The other woman, caught off guard, had backed up with each advancing accusation.

"Wishes, humph!" Sophronia said. "I have five children. Five. I have heard every story about wishes ever told, including the ones with djinn. Even when the wish comes true, it always gets twisted, causing more harm than good. That's why you tell the story, to teach your children that they can't just wish for fortune; they have to *earn* it." And she stalked back to the cart.

"True," the woman conceded. Rather than being quelled, she seemed even more interested and strolled around the front of the cart, absently patting Luki. "Rash people who make wishes they haven't thought through often get such a lesson. But you are not rash." Her voice was silk. "You already work so hard. For you the reward would be deserved." She perched on the edge of the well, swinging her feet like a child.

"Just for fun," she cajoled lightly, "I'm very curious what yours would be. There must be something you've wished you could have."

Sophronia sighed, shaking her head, the long list of chores and errands running through her mind. She didn't have time to chat about wishes. Then she laughed.

"With five kids, you know what I'd wish for?" It was absurd, but she had, on occasion, wished for something. "For the next ten years, every time I said the magic word, I'd suddenly have two extra arms and hands appear so I'd have four instead of two, and then with another magic word I could make them disappear again. Oh and no one looking at me would be able to see them; they'd just think I was really dexterous."

The strange woman laughed with a genuine, infectious amusement.

"I have never heard a more well thought out and useful wish. If that is all you wish for, then you are a wise woman indeed."

"I don't know about wise," Sophronia scoffed. "After all, I'm the one with five children and a husband at sea more than he's home. But yes, it's what I sometimes wish I had."

"And what would be your magic word?"

"Huh," she grunted. "Exasperated. It's my usual state of being."

"And the word to make them go?"

"I don't know," she shrugged. "How about done?" Playing along with the fantasy seemed the only way to get the woman to leave. And, truth be told, it was nice to imagine.

"Where is your coin?" a beguiling whisper by her ear. When had the woman moved from the well?

Sophronia's hand reached into her pocket of its own volition and pulled out the strange coin.

"Toss it in the well. You never know." The woman's sly, mischievous look made Sophronia feel like one of her children playing a secret game. She tossed the coin and heard the splash in the water at the bottom, then she turned back, laughing a little at herself.

"I guess that's . . . " she stopped, spinning all the way around. The woman was gone, the square deserted. Sophronia's face flushed at her foolishness.

"Daydreaming when I have work to do," she chided herself, further glad that little Rezi and Iason had slept through the whole thing. Guiding the cart up to the well, she put the incident out of her mind.

Upon arriving home, Sophronia was greeted by a bouncing and dancing Lysandra.

"Papa's ship has been spotted off Skiathos. He'll be home on tomorrow's eventide!"

Sophronia's heart skipped a beat. She so missed Calix on his long voyages. Each return renewed their passion as though they'd just married. She'd been heavily pregnant with little Rezi when he'd left; now the baby was half a year old.

Sophronia had just finished shifting the water urns into place when Rezi awoke, howling to be fed, which woke her brother, who immediately started fussing at the sudden onslaught next to him. She picked up the baby and got her into the sling at her breast, which immediately calmed her. Iason was another matter.

"Come on, sweeting," she said, taking his hand to lead him to a bench to sit beside her. She put her free arm around him, and he snuggled against her. He just needed a little mama time to adjust out of sleep.

"Give it back!" Vasos hollered in the next room.

"Make me," came Kiril's sneer, and Sophronia groaned, closing her eyes.

"Sometimes," she whispered as the argument escalated to include Lysandra, "I am just so exasperated with you three."

Sophronia's shoulders tingled oddly. She scowled, then her eyes widened as she felt hands resting on both hips under her clothes. She looked down at her right arm supporting Rezi and her left arm around Iason.

Panic rose in her. Breathe, she scolded herself; do not upset the children.

As she calmed, she remembered the incident at the well.

Impossible.

But the sensible argument warred with what she could feel. She concentrated on the additional limbs, raising and lowering them slightly, encumbered as they were within the cloth. Then she attempted to tickle Iason with the left one. He giggled. One more test.

"Away," she said under her breath.

Nothing happened. No, that wasn't it. What had she said?

"Done."

The tingling returned briefly, and the limbs disappeared. She almost laughed out loud. Iason, recovered and ready to play, jumped down and went off in the direction of the now seemingly negotiated fight. Sophronia switched Rezi to her left breast.

Can this be real?

"Exasperated," she whispered and felt the second set of arms return. "Done." The limbs disappeared, and she clapped a hand over her mouth in delight.

Blessed Mary, it *is* real!

She would have to adjust her sleeves to allow the limbs freedom, but that would be easy.

"Exasperated." she said again in her room after Rezi was burped, cleaned, and set down to play at the foot of the bed. She slowly pulled the new limbs out and examined them. They seemed to use her shoulders alongside the original ones. They wanted to follow the motions of her natural limbs, so getting them to act independently would take practice. She was just wondering if anyone would be able to see them when the voices of her arguing-again children got closer and louder.

"Vasos pulled my hair," wailed Lysa, running into the room.

"You took my soldier!" Vasos countered on her heels.

"You and Kiril were ganging up on my queen," accused Lysa, and she punched Vasos in the arm. After an angry shriek of pain, Vasos retaliated. The scuffle knocked Iason, who'd followed out of curiosity, into the wall. He bumped his head and started crying.

Sophronia picked up Iason with her natural arms then used her new ones to pull Lysandra and Vasos apart.

"Enough!" she scolded while simultaneously soothing Iason. "Lysandra, kitchen. Vasos, courtyard. Both swept and washed. Now!"

Their puffed up anger sagged into limp resignation at the tone of her voice, and they shuffled off. She brought a third hand up to Iason's head and stoked his hair. The three year old had stopped crying, and she looked into his face.

"All better?" She asked. He nodded, then looked quizzically at her. She realized he could feel three hands on him. Could he see them? The older children hadn't seemed to, but maybe really young ones could. She put her fourth hand up, finger to her lips, and said, "Shhh. Our secret, okay?"

Iason giggled and nodded. She put him down, and he skipped off.

"Well, that was helpful." Sophronia picked up the mirror near her bed, turning side to side.

"Astounding," she said. "I thought they were all just stories."

She thought of the consequences occurring in some of the djinn stories, many quite dire and with tragic outcomes. The woman had called her wish well thought out. Of course, she hadn't been desperate like most of the story wishers, although clearly the djinn at least thought her gullible. Some of the stories were lessons in greed, and maybe those folks deserved what they got; but others were not. People in no frame of mind to think through the wisdom of their desires did not deserve horrible fates. And who did the djinn think they were to pass such judgment? Tales of morality were one thing; having them real was quite another. And to what purpose?

Sophronia walked out to the garden at the rear of the house. She began straightening up the pots and urns, but not being particularly careful. After a few moments, the hair on her arms stood up, and she distinctly felt eyes on her, although she appeared to be alone.

The new arms knocked into things unless she concentrated on how to use them. Every time pottery shattered on the stones, she heard faint musical laughter. She made a point of muttering, mildly cursing, and looking genuinely frustrated. After a while she sighed, seeming to give up, and sat down.

"Done," she said. "This is impossible."

Pretty soon she felt the presence leave.

So, she thought, *apparently when I use my wish, I'm entertainment. That's interesting. And quite disturbing.*

She walked back into the house, mentally cataloging every djinn story she knew. There was a way to fix this; she just had to find the right story.

After inspecting the kitchen and the courtyard, she released Vasos and Lysandra. For most of the afternoon, there was relative peace in the house. Then Lysandra's shriek of terror sent Sophronia running for the garden.

Kiril stood at the base of the walnut tree. "I'm sorry," he pleaded, fear in his eyes. "I never meant for her to go so high."

Sophronia looked up. And up. Lysa was three quarters of the way to the top, clinging to a branch too weak to support her weight. Her feet wildly dangled, and every movement cracked the base of the branch further. There was a strong branch directly below Lysa, but it was too far down to safely drop to it. If she didn't land on it just right, she'd hit hard and fall to the ground.

"Exasperated," Sophronia whispered, kicking off her sandals. She started climbing four-armed up the other side of the tree until she could move across to the branch directly below her daughter.

A final crack jerked Lysa's grip loose, and she dropped. With her right two hands, Sophronia gripped the trunk barely in time to catch Lysa in a two-handed grip with the left pair. Sophronia leaned against the trunk, shaking, as Lysa sobbed in her arms. After a few minutes the two climbed down.

"What were you doing up there?"

Scared honest, Kiril answered. "I dared her," he said miserably. "She said she was a better climber and I dared her to prove it." He looked at his sister, who was still wiping tears. "I'm sorry. I didn't want you to get hurt."

"Done," Sophronia whispered.

"Mama, you were amazing!" Lysa said, turning to her.

"I didn't know you could climb trees," added Kiril.

She shook her head and smiled. "I was your age once. And mothers can do amazing things to save their children." She pulled them both to her, hugging them close.

"Now," she said sternly, looking into each face in turn, "have you two learned your lesson? No more dares!"

"No more dares," they both said earnestly.

Sophronia had just settled a sleepy Rezi after their evening meal when she overheard the others discussing the eventful day and peeked in the room.

"I thought I was going to die," Lysa said to Vasos's rapt attention.

"But Mama saved you," he said.

"Yes. She climbed so fast and just snatched me out of the air."

"I couldn't believe it, and I watched it happen!"

"But how did she do it, Kiril? How did she catch me and still hold on?"

"I don't know. It was all kind of a blur; she just did."

Iason giggled in the corner, and Sophronia knew he would never be able to keep her secret. Better to tell them herself. But later. Right now she had something else to do before nightfall.

"Kiril, Lysa, I need to go out for just a little while. Can I trust you to be responsible and care for the little ones without arguing?"

"Yes, Mama," they said.

Sophronia could feel herself being watched as she paced four-armed around the well. She'd remembered the right story and knew there was only one way to get this to go as she wanted.

"So, djinn, are you going to show yourself or just keep laughing at me from the shadows?"

"You needn't be so testy," came the musical voice from behind her.

"My supposedly well thought out wish, which I wasn't even actually making, as I recall, still has glitches."

"Even a wisher as careful as you can't think of everything."

"You tricked me."

The woman shrugged and smiled. "Maybe a little."

"It's what you djinn do. You prey on vulnerable people who are down on their luck, offering them every desire without any intention of truly helping them with what they really need."

"You make us sound evil. We are not responsible for the carelessness of mortals," she said loftily.

"Ah, but you withhold information. You know the harm a poorly considered wish can cause, yet you don't warn your victims."

"Of course not," the woman dismissed. "Where would be the fun then?"

"Finding enjoyment in the difficulties of others is evil."

"Your opinion."

"How long have you been doing this to people?"

"Me? Oh, hundreds of years, maybe more. I lose track. Time can be rather meaningless when one is as long-lived as we djinn. Hence the need for diversion from those who learn our valuable lessons."

"Well, you'll get no more entertainment from me. I will stop using the trigger word."

"And give up what saved your daughter? I don't think so."

"I managed before," she shrugged. "I'll manage again."

The djinn scowled. "You think you can avoid saying your word forever?"

"No, but I can for ten years. Remember? I put a limit on my wish."

The djinn stared, studying Sophronia, then laughed and shrugged.

"You know, I believe you can. Oh well, I've had my fun. It was the most unusual wish I have ever granted. Here," she tossed another silver coin to Sophronia, whose eyes narrowed suspiciously as she caught it. "I grant you one more wish. You can use it to take back your first wish," and she wiggled her fingers at Sophronia. "That's what most people do, although some fools do try to correct their first wish. It never ends well."

Sophronia smiled, stepping up to the well.

"I will learn to deal with the consequences of my choices," she said. "But since you've granted me a second wish, I will take you up on it. It's time for your kind to learn something, too."

The djinn's smiled disappeared as Sophronia held her closed fist over the water.

"I wish for all djinn to become mortal, ordinary humans with no magical powers."

The woman's eyes widened in horror, and she futilely lunged forward as Sophronia opened her hand and the coin dropped.

"And that, my dears," Sophronia said, having gathered all but Rezi on Kiril's bed to tell them the whole story, "is why there are no more djinn in the world."

"Wow," Lysa said, "but you kept your wish?"

"Exasperated," she whispered and pulled them into her four arms. "Yes," she said, "and this is their best use."

Sophronia hugged her precious children to her, randomly wondering if Calix's return would add yet another. Maybe she should have wished for six arms.

"All right, you four. Into bed and stay there."

After tucking them in, Sophronia continued to experiment with the new limbs. She just had to stay more conscious of where the additional arms were. Yes, she could handle ten years of just about anything. She'd have to tell Calix, although it might be fun to wait. Her face flushed at the thought of embracing her husband with four arms.

"I told you three to stay in bed," she said without turning to see Kiril,

Lysandra, and Vasos trying to sneak past. Their deflation was palpable.

"Did you wish for eyes in the back of your head, too?" Asked Vasos plaintively.

"Of course not," she answered, turning to them and smiling. "All mothers have those."

POWER PLAY
by
Cat Greenberg

This is the third reprint story, appearing as it originally did in Sword & Sorceress XI, *published in 1994.*

The spell was holding; barely, but it was holding. Calia walked past the last guard unseen and slipped into Prince Jevan's bed chamber.

Please don't let it fade now! She thought. Naked as she was (since the lotion worked only on flesh), it would be embarrassing if she became visible again anywhere in the palace but here in *this* room . . . Nothing would save her if it happened here. Knowing Jevan, he'd probably get a good laugh out of suddenly finding her this way in his chambers—that is, right before he killed her.

The *nerve* of that bastard, suggesting she'd do better as a harlot than the sorceress she was, then forcibly offering to initiate her himself! She'd barely gotten away in one piece let alone with her precious virginity, on which all her spells depended.

Well, we'll see who laughs after tonight, won't we?

She crept toward the huge bed where the prince lay sprawled on his back beside one of his concubines. The sheets were pulled aside, her target wide open.

How lucky can I get?

Calia carefully opened the pouch she'd been hiding in her fist and sprinkled the contents lightly over Jevan's groin. The powder sparkled briefly, then disappeared.

I hope she was memorable, she thought viciously. *She'll be your last!*

Jevan stirred, and Calia stepped backward. Her eyes strayed to a wall mirror, and panic gripped her throat. She was materializing! And Jevan was waking up! Gods, not here!

Jevan sat up and looked straight at Calia. The sleepy confusion on his face quickly turned to anger, and he bellowed for the guards.

Calia shrank back against the wall. Looking down at her rapidly appearing self, she muttered the spell again, but she only half faded. Why wasn't it working?

Gods and Goddesses! If any of you are real, you can have anything; just get me out of here!

Done, she heard, or thought she heard.

She looked up at the opening door, just as the guards burst into the room. That did it—she was good as dead. She squeezed her eyes shut, not really wanting to see the blow she knew was coming, but they rushed right past her, as though . . . She opened one eye and looked down, then quickly clamped her hand to her mouth to stifle her cry of relief. The spell was working again!

She didn't wait, afraid the spell might still falter. She ran out of the room and down the corridor as Jevan howled angry orders, trying to convince his guards that someone really *had* been in his room. She reached the top of the stairs and raced down them three and four at a time, hit the bottom floor, and bolted for the door (barely missing the guard who was entering), then ran across the courtyard and into the street, around the corner, into an alley, down another alley, and finally up the three flights of outside stairs to her own rooms. Calia slammed the door shut, slipped the bolt into place, and slid to the floor, panting.

She remembered to break the spell, then just sat there on the floor, slowly regaining her wits and her breath. Her side hurt and her head pounded something awful, but she was alive—and she'd *done* it!

"Yes, you have."

Calia jerked up her head at the sound of a male voice, staring with renewed panic—and complete bewilderment—at the elegantly clad young man sitting on her bed. She swallowed hard and slowly got to her feet, sliding up against the door, then realized she was still naked and cursed under her breath. The furnishings were sparse in the best of times, and there was nothing she could conveniently grab for cover, so she clothed herself with the only thing she did have—her dignity—and refused to acknowledge any discomfiture to this intruder, who'd somehow managed to get past warding spells that were *supposed* to be unbreachable.

Unless, of course, he was a sorcerer.

Damn.

Today was really not going very well.

What next? She wondered silently.

"Paying me for getting you out of Jevan's palace would be a good start. You did say I could have anything."

Calia's mouth dropped open. *No one* could have known of her plan. "How did you . . . " she started, then scowled at him. "Who are you?" she demanded.

"The god who answered your prayer, of course. Were you expecting someone else?" he asked innocently, then burst into astonished laughter. "You really *don't* believe we exist, do you? Oh, I assure you I'm quite real. Here," he said, rising and taking a step toward her. "Touch me; you'll see."

Calia's eyes narrowed as she folded her arms across her chest and pointedly ignored the offered hand. He shrugged and sat back down, obviously still amused. *She* wasn't. *She* was furious.

She was also more than a little unnerved by this—person—being where no one was supposed to be able to get and alluding to things *absolutely* no one but her should know.

"Okay," she said finally in very measured tones. "Let's say, just for the sake of argument, that I believe you. What, precisely, is your fee?"

Either he was a very good illusionist, or his smile actually did add light to the room. She shook herself inwardly. He was disconcertingly handsome, with gold-tinged, deep copper curls above a finely chisled face. And he sat in a way that showed he knew exactly what effect that perfectly cut velvet jacket, highlighting that lean, muscular frame of his would have on the average woman.

But then, Calia certainly did *not* consider herself an average woman. She'd spent ten years never allowing *any* man to attract her attention, always staying carefully aloof and disinterested. Virgin Witchcraft demanded that even her thoughts be untainted by physical lust and drew its limited power from the discipline of the user's restraint. For this man to disturb that hard-won discipline so much—it was exceedingly hard to keep from staring at him—severely bothered her.

Not man, Calia, she thought to herself. *He has the unfair advantage of being a god. Or so he claims. But how else could he have known?*

"Exactly," he said, and she glared at him.

"Stay out of my head!" *Damned telepathic eavesdropper.*

He was unperturbed. "In exchange for having saved your life," he said, then paused, looking her straight in the eye, "I ask for the sacrifice of your virginity."

"What!" Now his eyebrows did rise. Even a seasoned mercenary might have blushed at the colorful and exceedingly personal string of curses she flung at him before he could raise his hands to stop her.

"Please!" he said, hand to his chest in feigned shock. "Such ugly words from such a lovely mouth. I don't think I can bear it. If you'll kindly let me explain?"

She glared again but didn't resume the tirade.

"I've been watching you a long time,

Calia. You've got a tremendous amount of talent. But you're wasting it with the lesser magics. The witch who said they were the best you could do lied. Nemet knew your potential and was jealous of it. So she lied and convinced you that you were no better than she."

Calia was suspicious but was intrigued in spite of herself. She thought back to the night she'd come to Nemet, the oldest and most feared witch in this part of the city. How she'd confided to Nemet, and no one else, the power she felt growing within her, and a twelve-year-old girl's romantic dream of sorceress love unleashing it. It was what all the old stories said would happen. The stories whispered for centuries among the womenfolk when their men retired to their pipes and fires and the women were left alone. She'd memorized every word of every secret story and came to Nemet that night, her head filled with the promise of them. So Nemet had tested her. Calia hadn't understood the shock and anger that had shown briefly on the old woman's face before she told Calia that her feelings were false.

"You'll never have more than the powers of the Virgin Crafts, girl," she'd said. "Better satisfy yourself with that and forget the Passion Magics."

Now he said Nemet had lied? It could explain a lot of things. *If* he was telling the truth. And *if* he was what he claimed. But how else could he have known so much about her life?

"I'd like to show you what you're truly capable of, Calia," he continued, and Calia listened, interest and hope edging out her suspicion and anger. "You see, I'm still a relatively young god—more of a demigod, actually—and as such, I need more than just mindless followers, although those never hurt. I also need allies. Like a powerful sorceress. I want you to be my ally, Calia. I can help you unleash the power you've craved for so long—yes, it is within you. *And* I can teach you how to use it, better than any sorcerer could. He paused and leaned forward. "But you have to *want* it, Calia."

Her chin lifted slightly at what she had a feeling was meant as an insult. He was baiting her, but she wasn't nibbling—yet.

"Do you know how many women of your kind are capable of True Magic and never fulfill their potential? More than you think. Do you know why? The *real* reason why? Because *desire* is needed—an intense, passionate desire for power—and women, especially those who show magical talent, are taught to deny desire. They don't want to have to share their status, their control. And most women are reluctant to risk their comfortable niches. So they teach you *not* to want more than they hand you. They tell you that wanting more is wrong.

"The secret myth you grew up with is that a sorcerer releases the power in a mage-gifted woman. The truth is, you release the power *yourself* when you embrace the desire for it and abandon the restraints you've been taught."

He relaxed then, reclined, and leaned on one elbow.

"It can be a long and profitable alliance for both of us, not to mention a pleasurable one." He patted a spot on the bed next to him.

Calia chewed on her lip, thinking. He sounded sincerely reasonable—or he was just damned convincing. Maybe both. It certainly was an awful lot of trouble to go to if all he wanted was a tumble in the sheets. And the part about being taught never to desire was certainly true. More powerful than the old witch had said she could be? And if he wasn't the one who'd gotten her out of Jevan's palace (she wasn't *entirely* convinced, even though it seemed a logical conclusion), how could he know about her impromptu prayer?

"*Do* you want the power, Calia? Do you desire True Magic enough to free yourself of *their* restrictions?"

It was a risk, but what had playing it safe gotten her? A dingy room three floors above the blacksmith, that's what.

"Yes," she answered, looking him straight in the eye and walking resolutely over to the bed.

"Do I at least get to know your name?" she asked.

"Xander," he answered, pulling her down to kiss her.

They lay entwined on the bed as the sun broke through the night. Calia had barely slept; she was too delighted at how she felt. Amazing how years of lies could be wiped out so easily. She could feel the power tingling inside. *Her* power. Power many more like her could have if someone had the sense to tell them to take it. Enticing thought, that.

Xander stirred, waking, and reached for her. They kissed slowly, then he looked up at her.

"Disappointed?" he asked.

"Not in the least," she said. "But I do have one question. If gods in general do exist, how is it that you, and not some other god or goddess, answered me? *I* certainly wasn't being specific. Were you the only god in the vicinity or something?"

"But of course," he said, giving her a mischievous grin. "Why do you think your spell failed in the first place?"

CHAMELEON
by
Cat Greenberg

Sometimes when we write, it's a form of therapy. The first drafts of this story were written in 2008. I was going through a devastating divorce and felt helpless, my self esteem at its lowest, as I watched my life careening out of my control. Writing a character with self confidence to spare was therapeutic. She was also a fun character to write, and my first novelette. I hope you enjoy reading about her as much as I did writing her.

Oriah didn't need to join the crowd jostling to glimpse Castille Station through the single portage viewport. The anticipation of a hundred desperate people crashed over her with the ebb and flow of a planet-side ocean. She breathed in the emotion-charged air, lingering over the sharp taste of it. There were beings who came from the far side of the galaxy who actually lived off the emotions of lesser creatures, converting it to energy. Oriah sighed, preferring the sensations as a vice rather than a vitamin.

Someday she would go to one of the boarder stations on the edge of human space. It would be interesting to experience a nonhuman. Only the boarder stations mixed the various space-faring species—carefully—to avoid intergalactic war. The interior was solidly human.

The thud and clank of docking brought a change—sharp anticipation became laced with the bittersweet tang of anxiety: desperate people hoping this would be the place to find work or freedom or escape from whatever trouble they were fleeing. The passengers began to nervously busy themselves, collecting up belongings and small children, checking their passport chips. Not that they'd be out anytime soon; it would be at least an hour before the lower hatch opened on the downside of the station. The first- and second-class passengers, who disembarked to the upside decks, always came first. Stupid, really. Most of the people around Oriah arrived with little more than the clothes on their backs. If downsiders came out first, they'd be processed before the upsiders finished collecting their considerable hand luggage.

Oriah slowly pulled in one last surge, sending subtly soothing waves in return, before retreating to the alcove she had made her home during the voyage. She closed off her mind to the din and reached into her pack for her own passport chips. Who would she play the game as on Castille? She clicked through them one at a time. Mysterious Yasimi? No, she'd been Yasimi on the previous station. Scholarly Ingrid? Hmmm, no, she really wasn't in a scholarly mood. Ah, yes! Pallas Lang! She was definitely in the mood for Pallas's kind of fun. Flame haired, green eyed, flashy and flamboyant Pallas.

She chuckled and pulled on a dingy scarf, assuming her usual disembarking identity, then smudged her face with the ever-present grime of this compartment to hide her age. Pallas had to wait until she had a room to use. For now, she was simply another forgettable downsider nobody.

Oriah was very good at her game because she so enjoyed playing it. She wasn't totally unknown to the fools at the psychic registry, or to the various casinos she visited. Several people were fully aware of her existence; they were simply unable to connect any two of her identities, let alone all nine of them, to pin her down.

As far as Oriah was concerned, they could stay in the dark forever. She had no use for a registry of moribund bureaucrats trying to keep tabs on every telepath in the Sol Association. Of course, the goal was to make the registry mandatory, indenturing any telepath who couldn't pay its expensive and profitable licensing fees. The bureau was using pushing the politicos that direction and already the media were beginning to call unregistered telepaths rogues.

Well, rogue did rather accurately describe her, but it had nothing to do with her being unregistered at the bureau.

It took nearly two hours for the upper classes to finish and the port authority to open the lower decks. Oriah's chip showed a poor resolution image of a nondescript woman in her forties to the bored guard. She barely touched his mind, only the slightest pressure to bend his perception of her so the match he expected to see is what registered. The guards assigned to the portage deck were easy marks, never the bright, promotion-seeking stars who got the plum topside jobs.

Once through customs, the game began. She slipped quietly into a public sanitation closet for her first change. She emerged clean faced in a khaki jumpsuit and cap, straight brown hair tied in a short tail at the nape of her neck. She looked like every other gray-collar station worker. Spying the lodging clerk's desk, she unzipped the top of the jumpsuit just a bit and pulled out yet another identity before getting in line.

"Aye, Lenni!" she said, spying his name badge as she reached the desk. His surface thoughts were of his last post on Artréal Station. "I ain't seen you since

Artréal!"

Caught off guard, he stammered. "Do, do I know you?"

"Now don' tell me I was that forgettable. Y'all hurt my feelin's, Lenni. Course, mebe' you don't remember too good, eh? Considerin' how much we drank!" She slapped his shoulder playfully, leaning on the counter to push her generous cleavage well into view. That did it! He started thinking about the partying he'd done on Artréal. One particular incident the night before he left was just hazy enough, including a vague but not unpleasant memory of a dark-haired woman. Oriah did like beginning the game with a stroke of luck.

"Ya said you were out celebratin' your transfer? Couldn't wait to get outta' tha' dump of a station?"

"Oh, yeah, um," he said, laughing and surreptitiously looking down at her chip, "Kate!" He pulled off the fake recognition with admirable sincerity.

"There ya go! Not so forgettable after all." She nudged him suggestively. "Not after the night we spent, eh, luv? Maybe we could, ya know, relive some old

233

times? You are still one fine lookin' man!" She had not failed to notice the shiny new wedding ring on his left hand.

"Oh, well," he said, flustered by her flirtations, "not a swinger no more, Kate. Got myself married last month." He quickly processed her papers, billeting her far from himself, thinking it was an area nice enough to keep her friendly but not too nice to give her the wrong idea about favors owed. By now some in the line were beginning to grumble.

"My loss, luv," she added with a suggestive wink.

"It was nice seeing you again, Kate. I gotta get back to work."

She shrugged and waved at him as she walked away, looking at the map on the billet card, like every other new grubber. Inwardly she smiled at her success and the elevated ego she'd given him. And she hadn't completely deceived him; he *was* one fine-looking man.

The modest cabin Lennie had assigned her was on Level BA6. Not too generous, after all. There were eight Below Axis levels, and the slums began at BA7. No matter. Pallas would get much better billeting.

Uriah pulled a long, hooded brown cloak from her pack plus her favorite gown, hung them in the steam cabinet and pushed start. She showered, then sat down on the floor in a loose robe, legs tucked under her. Closing her eyes, she turned her mind inward. Her awareness went deep, past the mere physical, all the way to the cellular, where she began the intricate adjustments to lighten her skin, ever so slightly, then adjust her hair's color and texture as she accelerated its growth. Thin, straight, dark hair moved past her shoulders as thick copper curls tumbled down. Coming back out of the deep, she cut off the black ends and tossed her new locks.

Hair and skin weren't difficult; eyes were another matter. They could be changed, but a stray thought could cause permanent damage. Besides, her gray eyes made using lenses easy. Digging into her pack, she brought out the compact that held her array of lenses and selected the deeper green ones.

blind spot directly below it. She moved toward the area as the lift doors opened on AA1. To anyone watching the feed, it looked as if the woman in the brown cloak exited the lift at the first Above Axis level.

A couple entered, completely wrapped up in conversation, and absently hit the AA3 button. The lift doors opened on AA2, and a security guard entered and hit the AA4 button. Not what Oriah wanted. His surface thoughts were of a recent argument with his partner, and he rocked on his heels, muttering to himself. Oriah kept her back to him. As the lift approached AA3, she nudged his irritation up a notch, inserting into his mind the visual of him getting off the lift. The door opened, and the couple left, followed by the preoccupied guard, whom she gently steered into the path of the group waiting to get on the lift. Not looking, he plowed into the woman at the front. The lift doors closed on the ensuing apologetic commotion.

Oriah slipped off the cloak while mentally reaching into the lift controls, slowing its progress slightly. She unfastened the lining and pulled the cloak inside-out. Ignorable brown became attention-getting iridescence, the diamond-dust treated material throwing off sparkles of silver and gold rainbows. She released the lift, which glided to a stop at AA4. When the doors opened, she moved into view of the recorder behind the first person to get on, fooling the vid into thinking she'd just arrived in the car from the beginning of the first-class residences. To the distracted passengers, she was just one of the many who got on, although a couple of them were mildly surprised that they hadn't noticed her waiting with them. With a little help, they quickly lost that train of thought.

At AA7, a shimmering cloud in four-inch heels glided from the lift—Pallas always makes an entrance to remember. The loose hood perfectly framed her copper curls as the billowing cloak floated on her shoulders. Heads turned appreciatively as she passed. The casino's pandemonium of colored lights reflected on the material, and it winked and dazzled as she flipped off the hood and swept the cloak from her shoulders.

She handed it to the checker, whose eyes grew round with amazement at the soft fabric. The girl handed Pallas a claim token, still looking at the cloak. Pallas caught her hand, bringing the girl's attention back, then winked as she slid a credit chit across the tip box.

"Take good care of her, Molly," she told the attendant. The box registered a tip just large enough to give the hope of extreme generosity upon her return.

The attendant smiled and curtsied. "Oh, I will, Ma'am," she said in the faint cockney accent that gave away her Brunswick Station roots. "I certainly will!"

Points for the curtsey, thought Oriah.

Next she stopped at the security station to be scanned for electronics, raising her arms and swirling the dress as the middle-aged gentleman ran a scanner up and down. She waggled her eyebrows at his stoically bored countenance.

"Jerry," she said—rule number one: always notice the name badge. "Where would I put it?" Her teasing finally caught his eye. Oriah had mastered the art of an infectious grin by the time she was thirteen.

"You'd be surprised, ma'am," he said, just the hint of a smile showing through. "You're good to go."

"Oh, I hope I'm much better than good," she flirted. "How are the tables here?"

"Reasonable." It was the standard answer. Then, just as she was walking away, he added, "Watch out for Marty on table seven. He's our winningest dealer, and he don't like women."

Pallas smiled warmly, "Thanks, Jerry." She felt his mood shift, a little more upbeat than before.

She waltzed up to the cashier. "Five hundred, Ajani darling," she purred, handing a credit chit to the young man at the window. She looked straight into his eyes, giving him a sensuous smile. She didn't need telepathy to know his knees had just turned to jelly as he stammered and punched buttons to dispense her chips. As he pushed them toward her, she grabbed his tie, pulled him to her, and kissed him lightly.

"For luck," she whispered, enjoying the bemused look that lingered on his face as she turned away.

That was three whose day she'd brightened. Good karma in the bank. Now to brighten her credit account.

The man who'd been watching Pallas on and off for the past three hours walked over to the dice table and stood at her elbow, a carefully schooled look of passive interest on his face as she glanced around, laughing. She felt a twinge of pressure in her mind, an oh, so subtle probe. She felt him push skillfully, prodding along her barriers, looking for any weakness to let him past.

A challenge, she thought, picking up the dice for another roll.

So, did he work for the casino? Or was he a rogue like her? Not that being one would make him any less dangerous. There was no honor among rogues; self-interest always came first, especially among gamblers. She'd learned that lesson the hard way.

Coming up against her barriers told him she had an extraordinarily disciplined mind. This did not necessarily clue him into her being a telepath. Professional gamblers had equally well-disciplined minds since they ran the risk of coming against either a rogue or, in some of the seedier regions of space, a registered telepath who gambled on behalf of the casino. Not illegal, but the classier establishments eschewed the practice as contemptible, saying they won gamblers money the old-fashioned way—stacked odds and strong liquor. Of course, in Oriah the man had unknowingly found both a rogue *and* a professional gambler. The probing stopped as he went to stand a little way down the table.

Time for someone else to win, she thought, flicking the dice and giving the barest nudge so a six came up instead of the needed seven. Unlike some in her place, she never used her psi gift to win. Her parents, both professional gamblers themselves, instilled that into her as soon as her abilities manifested.

"A true gambler does not use such an unfair advantage," her mother had said. "Cheating comes in many forms, all of them unprofessional."

The crowd shouted disappointment, but Pallas just shrugged. Another woman picked up the dice as Pallas scooped her remaining chips into her small bag and headed to the bar. The woman rolled, and Oriah nudged the dice to eleven.

Pallas smiled at the bartender. "Orian Fizz, please, Mari." Not the most expensive champagne but one that did show a certain flare of taste.

Surreptitiously dropping a neutralizer into the flute, Pallas turned and leaned casually on the bar, raising the crystal to her lips.

The man who'd watched her caught her eye and raised his martini in salute. She smiled and nodded to him, signaling permission to approach.

At least this adversary was easy on the eyes. A little taller than her, with dark, expertly cut hair brushing his shoulders and an immaculate beard kept just on the civilized side of bushy.

"I'm Tanik," he said, taking her offered hand and kissing it as he bowed. "Tanik Sanovic."

Smooth, she thought, making no attempt to mask it. His mouth quirked up slightly higher than his warm smile.

"Pallas Lang," she acknowledged. "Pleased to meet you."

"You were quite impressive with the dice."

"Thank you. It was a good warm up. Still, wouldn't want the table to get stale." There was no reason to hide her gambling skill from him, only her psi gifts.

"Did you come in on the *Stargazer*?" He named a cruise ship that had docked opposite the *Celestine*, which she had come in on.

She shrugged. "Perhaps. I really don't pay attention to names. The destination, now that's something to pay attention to. Castille sounded interesting, and my companion had passage booked, so I tagged along."

"Companion?" She felt the skillfully gentle probe again. A feather touch to her barriers.

"Long gone," she waved her fingers dismissively. "We parted ways just before docking. He became distracted by a brunette."

"Unfortunate for him."

"How long have you worked for the casino?" she asked conversationally.

"Am I that obvious?" He was genuinely amused.

"I noticed you two hours ago, luv." She twirled a finger at him, pointing to his lack of bulging pockets. "No chips. Either you've lost everything, or you haven't gambled once. You don't strike me as the type to lose everything. Don't feel bad, in this profession one gets exceedingly good at reading people. How else will I know what cards my opponents hold?"

"Ah, but I am officially off the clock and hold no cards." He spread his hands.

She laughed, lifting her glass. "So I see. Then how should I think of you?"

"You should think of me as the perfect guide for a stroll through the Hydro-sphere." He extended his arm.

Oh my, he was good. She sensed no guile. He was genuinely fascinated and seemed a decent sort, most definitely easy on the eyes. He even smelled good. She just needed to know one more thing.

"Why, Tanik," she purred, "I think you read my mind!"

Bingo. That got him to look away, ever so briefly, but he knew it had been just enough of a reaction to give himself away.

She stepped back, giving him a sardonic appraisal.

"Tanik! Are you one of those?"

He raised his hands in supplication.

"Guilty as charged." He pulled out an ID card. "Registered, Telepathic Security Services."

"Were you scanning me?" She raised her eyebrows as she took another sip.

"Only what's allowed, surface thoughts. Your mind is very disciplined."

"In this business, it's the first thing one learns if one wants to survive to make a living."

Pallas finished her champagne. Putting down the crystal flute, she came provocatively close.

"You," she said, poking his chest with one long manicured finger, "have been a very naughty boy."

He smiled down at her, radiating playfulness. "I can't promise not to do it again. After all, a man has only so much willpower against such a beautiful temptation."

"Well," she said, sliding her hand through his previously offered arm, "behave, and maybe I'll give you something worthy of the effort."

Pallas's quarters were a vast improvement over Kate's. Three rooms instead of one, luxurious lounge area, well-stocked bar, and plush bedroom with a grand view of the stars. Her winnings had been modest by Oriah's standards. They would increase tomorrow. Today had been just a bit of fun practice to pay beginning expenses and get a feel for the tables.

Tanik was certainly a charming addition to the game. The Hydro-sphere had been incredible—five levels of waterfalls and foliage. Tanik knew every species of flower. Once past the preliminary impression stage, they'd chatted amiably about stations they'd visited, a few planets. Both were space-born and less comfortable in gravity wells. Tanik gave up his probing, content to accept Pallas at face value.

She had to admit, at least to herself,

that she was of two minds about him. On the one hand, she was intrigued by the man he seemed to be. On the other hand, she was disgusted by his profession. He really didn't seem the type to be TSS. The practice of the registry using telepaths against each other was growing, especially in the powerful gaming industry, which offered substantial financial incentives. Yet, Tanik didn't act as though money was very important to him. There was something odd every time he tried to probe her. It would take time to tease it out without giving herself away. Was he worth the effort?

Oriah poured brandy into a glass, dropping in another neutralizer. It had been years since she'd last felt the effects of alcohol. Feeling attraction could be just as bad, and there was no neutralizer for that effect. She vividly remembered the aftermath of the first and last time she allowed her focus to be disturbed by the combination, with an untrustworthy partner who'd nearly got her spaced. Rule number two: never lose control of yourself or the situation. She'd escaped by random dumb luck—something not to be counted on twice.

"I think a shopping spree is in order," she said aloud and queried the concierge.

"Yes, ma'am," the young woman on duty answered. Oriah gave her Pallas's languorous smile.

"Hello, there. Taylor, isn't it?"

She beamed at being remembered. "Yes, ma'am."

"I feel like shopping, Taylor. Where can I shop at 0430?" She took a long sip of the harmless brandy.

"Promenade Three, ma'am."

"Thank you, Taylor. You're a dear."

There was another rule to her game which she believed inviolate: always make the hired help feel special and valued. First, because they deserved it, and, second, because you never knew when a friendly underling might be in a position to save your life.

Shopping spree completed, Pallas walked the corridors of the station. She had changed into the stylish white jumpsuit and delicately sequined floral boots she'd purchased. Oriah normally packed extremely light. She left most of her station purchases in the room when she left, with a parting note to the maid, saying, "Help yourself." But she would have to see if there was room to keep these boots. They were incredibly comfortable.

Continuing to wander aimlessly, she appeared to be another curious tourist. In fact, she was making a mental note of every lift, service access, and communications terminal she passed. She finished BA1, predominantly mid-class restaurants, then came strolling out of the lift on BA2, the medical bays. Always good to note their location.

She passed the first bay, security locked. Only pre-registered first-class residents had the access code. At this hour, no one needed medical attention. In five or six more hours, roughly midday station time, there would be many first-class hangovers for the bay personnel to treat.

Terror and grief slammed into Oriah, and she staggered, catching herself on the wall. A woman's voice pleaded from around the curve of the corridor.

"Please! You can't just leave him to suffer!"

Oriah listened, extending just enough of her awareness while walling out the extreme emotional onslaught.

"I know I'll find work soon. I will pay you. But I need the medicine for him now."

"I told you," the clerk said, annoyed. "No credit. Go home."

"Soltus disease becomes contagious as it progresses, I saw it enough on the rim. My daughter and I will be at risk if he isn't treated."

So will the rest of you BAX scum, Oriah picked up his broadcast thoughts. *Better to be rid of you.*

Oriah closed her eyes, calming her flaring temper. This woman had survived the Galax insurrection. She deserved better. Oriah heard the panel slam shut and felt the woman's stunned hopelessness.

Oriah moved slowly around the curve. She recognized the woman from the portage passengers on the *Celestine.* Her jumpsuit was clean but thread worn. A small girl stood shyly at her knee, clutching her mother's pant leg. What was left of the girl's shoes was held together with cargo tape.

The woman caught her breath, startled by Oriah's appearance.

"Forgive me," Pallas said. "I couldn't help overhearing. Is it your husband who is ill?"

"Yes, I . . . I'm sorry I disturbed you." She reached down to gather the little girl into her arms. Oriah put her hand out as the woman went to walk past her.

"You have nothing to apologize for, scrapper," she said, using the term of colloquial respect for a veteran of that brutal war. She sent her most soothing aura toward the two, one that instilled trust.

"You deserve better than that," Pallas said, nodding toward the window. "Were you a medic?"

"Yes."

"How far along is your husband?"

"He just progressed to stage two. In three days, he'll become contagious, just before . . ." She didn't want to finish the sentence in front of the little girl. Pallas didn't need to be a telepath to know the rest—just before he dies.

"What's your name?"

"Dina," she said hesitantly, "Dina Mitchell. This is Andria"

"Hello, Andria. I'm Pallas."

"Hello," Andria said in a small voice.

"You have very pretty eyes, Andria."

"Thank you," it was almost a whisper.

"It's a little scary with your daddy sick, isn't it?"

Andria nodded.

"I will get you the meds your husband needs," she told Dina. At the look on her face, Oriah added, "Legally; don't worry."

"Are you going to make my daddy well?"

Oriah smiled and brushed the girl's hair back. "I'm going to try."

Andria smiled back, then added in true child-priority fashion, "My birthday is tomorrow." She held up the appropriate fingers. "I'll be five years old."

"You will? That's a very special age, Andria."

"Uh-huh," Andria nodded importantly, and both women laughed.

"What's your favorite color, Andria?"

"Purple," Andria said, the fear beginning to recede. "What's yours?"

"Green," Pallas said, "but I like

purple, too. Especially purple shoes."

"I wish I had purple shoes," Andria said wistfully.

"Well, you go home with your momma, and once we take care of getting your daddy's medicine, maybe we can make that wish come true."

"Really?"

"Really. After all, five is a very important birthday."

There were tears in her mother's eyes, but behind them, the fear that her daughter was being given an empty promise. Oriah looked directly into those worried eyes.

"I don't make empty promises."

Dina's mouth opened then shut again. Oriah smiled.

"Go on now," she said. "Somebody's sleepy."

Pallas patted the girl's shoulder as she yawned hugely. Oriah sent another wave of reassurance and a gentle nudge to get her moving. Dina Mitchell gave Pallas a weak, unsure smile as she headed to the lift, hope beginning to bloom in her mind.

Oriah watched them leave, waiting for the lift to cycle before ringing the bell. The panel flew up violently.

"I told you no . . . " the clerk growled before realizing that this was not the woman he thought it was. His face fell, eyes wide.

"Well, I never!" Pallas began in her most indignant, and loud, voice. "Who is your supervisor?   I want to see them now!"

"I'm sorry," he stammered, glancing sideways, afraid someone would hear, "I thought . . . "

"You thought?"   Her voice a little more shrill. "I seriously doubt it!"

A middle-aged woman appeared in the window, and the clerk's fear went up a notch.

"I'm Dr. Flynn, the administrator here. Is there a problem?" She asked.

"I should say so," Pallas began, adding hurt to her indignation, "I came for help with this excruciating headache and this, this, person, attacked me. Refusing me service and yelling at me on top of it."   Tears filled her eyes, and Andy's mouth opened and closed as he tried to decide what to say.

"Andy?" Dr. Flynn prompted.

Oriah mentally nudged him. Time for

a little truth telling, Andy boy.

"I thought she was the BAX scum trying to get Soltus serum on credit," he said, unable to stop himself.

"Soltus? Is that what that poor woman in the lift was crying about?" Then Pallas gasped, "Isn't that contagious?"

"Explain yourself, Andy," Dr. Flynn said in a voice that brokered no argument. Under the glare of Dr. Flynn, the whole story came out, even his wish for the disease to kill most of the BAXers. Oriah hardly had to encourage him at all, just lower his inhibitions and let his bias have free reign.

Dr. Flynn was appalled. "You would put the entire station at risk to satisfy your PL bigotry? Not only are you fired, but the cost of the serum is coming out of your final pay."

Curt orders were given, and a medical team headed to the lift. Pallas accepted Dr. Flynn's apology and a mild analgesic for her "headache" and left, ignoring Andy's glare.

Over the course of the week, Pallas had consistently deflected Tanik's probes, giving him a hint of surface thought (mostly glimpses of her attraction to him), and Tanik seemed convinced that she was mindblind. However, Oriah knew deception could easily go both ways and never assumed hers was perfect. The day you got cocky was the day you got caught.

On duty, Tanik floated from table to table, always orbiting back to wherever Pallas played. Her dress was blue tonight, purchased with the third evening's winnings. She sat at the black jack table manned by the supposedly woman-hating Marty, a considerable pile of chips in front of her.

The table was shared by two young men to her right, amateurs both. The blond one had trouble concentrating every time Pallas shifted on her stool, but his ebony companion's fantasies were of dealer Marty. Both had the reckless air of playing with money they hadn't had to earn. The woman next to them was older, elegant and harder to read. She was not a pro yet, but she was training herself to be one. Still, her eyes gave away hope when she neared twenty-one, and she had only sporadic luck hiding her surface thoughts. Next to her there was an empty seat, then a gray-haired gentleman in an expensive tuxedo sat at first base. This one was a pro; his face and surface thoughts gave nothing away. He won as often as Oriah, and while he did enjoy the view, Pallas never disturbed his concentration.

The dealer completed the deal of cards to each player then himself. The pro received a nine of diamonds, the woman a six of clubs, and her two amateur tablemates a two of clubs and queen of spades, respectively. Pallas's first card was an ace of hearts, and Marty's up card was a ten of spades. The pro's second card was the ten of clubs, to which he nodded. The woman received a nine of hearts. Her jaw tightened briefly, then she was impassive again.

You're trying too hard, Pallas thought and glanced casually about. Tanik was safely on the other side of the room dealing with a drunk who was loudly unhappy about his losing streak. She sent a feather-light touch to the woman, a calming aura. Watch and learn, it encouraged anonymously, relax, enjoy the game. The change in the woman was only perceptible to Oriah. Not even the pro, who was definitely mind-blind, would have noticed. Only Oriah could feel the difference as the woman considered her cards. The first amateur received a jack of spades and his friend a seven of diamonds, who grumbled at his luck—too high to hit, too low to hold.

Pallas received another ace, this one diamonds. The two amateurs groaned appreciatively as Pallas smiled and pushed an identical bet forward to cover the split hand. The pro at the end gave a nod of respect to his acknowledged equal.

"A lovely pair, Marty. Thank you."

"Madame," he acknowledged, dealing two more up cards to her. The first was a five of diamonds; the second was a jack of spades.   "T w e n t y - one," he intoned.

Marty didn't actually hate women; he simply wasn't affected by them. However, Oriah knew his mutual interest in the amateur no matter how passive Marty's face.

Marty dealt his down card then went back to the pro at the end, who signaled he was staying. The near-pro signaled hit to the dealer. A five of hearts making twenty—she stayed, and only Oriah knew the happy relief the woman felt. Next the blond amateur signaled a hit to his twelve and received a ten of spades.

"Busted, again!" he said and signaled the server for another drink. "I'm gonna try the wheel, Gabe." And off he went.

His friend grinned at Marty, a suggestive look in his eyes, and said, "I think I'll stay."

Marty turned to Pallas with lifted spirits and flipped over a three of diamonds in response to her fingernail tapping on the remaining ace. Another tap produced a six of hearts. The next card had to be a six or less. She considered the previous hands and the cards already in play. She'd been at the table long enough for three of the decks in the shoe to be gone. She tapped the ace again, and Marty produced another ace.

"Damn!" came from Gabe, and Pallas deliberately allowed one eyebrow to rise before she tapped again—four of clubs.

"Hold," Pallas said.

"I should think so!"

Marty flipped over his down card, an eight of hearts.

"Eighteen. House holds. House wins two, pays four." Marty pulled in both amateur's chips then pushed stacks in front of each of the winning bets.

Pallas scooped up her winnings then leaned down to Gabe as she walked past.

"Marty's off at 0200," she whispered. His face lit up as she moved to one of the roulette tables.

Pallas pushed the lift button for BA7. Her vibrant hair coiled under a hat, her flashy dress traded for coveralls with ample pockets, a nondescript pack on her back. It was her third such sojourn since arriving.

The corridor she stepped into reeked of human refuse and sweat, mingled with blood and fear. These were the levels the casino owners didn't want patrons to see. In the casino, all was clean and bright, no need to see the dark and dirty side of station life. First-class passengers never bothered with the portage ones. These were the people with sparse choices left, opportunities becoming fewer the farther into space they went. To have nothing would be a step up for many of these people, who never realized it was possible to have less than nothing until it was too late.

Pallas approached an old man sitting in a crumpled, half-conscious heap.

"Daddy," she said gently, reaching into her pack and bringing out a small package of protein bars and two juice packets. She crouched down, touched his unshaven face gently, and the eyes cleared a bit in recognition. "I brought your favorite."

He gave her a beaming, vacant smile. "Carrie?" he said. "My girl, you came back."

"Of course, I did, Daddy. I said I would." The recognition began to fade from his eyes. "Eat your dinner, Daddy," she pressed a bar into his hand. The eyes registered a brief flash, and he began to eat mechanically. She patted his cheek and got up.

His name was Anthony Griffin. His mind was nearly gone; disease and malnutrition, age, probably a good amount of alcohol, all conspiring against him. He'd been a good man once, strong, vital—part of the construction crew that had built the station. Now he was thrown away by the very company who owed him their existence. It was disgusting.

He wouldn't live much longer, days maybe. The daughter he mistook Oriah for had died in a ship accident two years before. It'd been six years since Oriah's own parents had died the same way. She never had a chance to say goodbye. So she said it to old Tony. He would die thinking he had seen his daughter and believing he was loved. It was all she could do.

She stayed until he fell asleep, reaching into his mind to give him peaceful dreams.

As she approached res602, Andria came running out, jumping into Pallas's arms.

"Ms. Pally!" the girl squealed. "Thank you for my birthday present! I love my purple shoes!" The girl planted a kiss on Pallas's cheek then scrambled down and skipped backward. "Look how high I can jump!"

"You're welcome," Pallas smiled warmly, tapping the girl's nose with her finger as she pulled another item from the bag. "They match your jumpsuit."

The girl squealed again and gave Pallas another hug, then twirled and ran to her approaching mother.

"Look, Mama!"

Dina beamed gratitude, and Oriah gladly received the offered hug.

"Your husband is better?" Pallas asked.

"Yes! So much so. He's sleeping now, but the medics come daily to check his progress and say he will recover completely. Andria and I were both tested and cleared."

"That's wonderful!"

"Pallas, how can we ever repay you?"

"Unnecessary. I was glad I could help. That jerk should never have refused you."

Pallas pulled a commissary chit from her bag and gave it to Dina. "Take this until you find work. There's a month's worth of credit on it."

Dina's eyes welled with tears. "Thank you," she whispered, hugging Pallas again. "You are truly an angel."

"The tables have been generous to me. I'm just spreading the luck to those more deserving."

Oriah kept the visit short and moved on, making several other stops until her bag was empty.

Andy was waiting when the lift stopped at BA6. He was agitated and angry, looking at his credit chit. She looked down but sensed his eyes on her as the lift started. She wanted to deflect his attention, but with his concentration solely on her, she dared not try a mental push that might be sensed and give away what she was.

"You don't look like a BAXer," he said, and she shrugged. "In fact, you look kinda familiar." Oriah tried to move nearer to the door as he came up behind her. "I'm talking to you, BAXer."

The lift opened on BA5, and she maneuvered around a couple getting on to slip out as the doors started to close. She thought she'd escaped, but he hit the door button and followed. She walked quickly, trying not to run. Thankfully, the residential corridor was not empty. She could sense he was still behind her, but his surface thoughts were jumbled, trying to figure out who she was. There was another lift at the other end of the hall, and she reached for it, mentally pushing the call button and speeding its arrival.

The lift opened, and two men came out. They wore the same dockside jumpsuit and carried duffels, giving away their new arrival status. They had been arguing, their surface thoughts concerned with a debt to a rather disreputable entity.

The larger one, a muscular man of thirty years or so, bumped into Pallas, dislodging her hat. That did it. Andy saw the red hair, and recognition clicked. Oriah slipped into the lift and closed the doors, interrupting the signal from the call button when he pushed it. The blind rage in his mind left her panting from thc effort to block it. She secured the hat and pushed every floor on the controls so he would have no way of being certain where she got off.

Back in her room, Oriah's hands shook as she poured herself brandy and, for the first time in years, briefly considered not putting a neutralizer in. She took several deep breaths, then pulled up the ship schedule as she sipped the harmless drink. There was a cruise ship leaving in six hours. Not the best choice. Sixteen hours for a cargo ship with some passenger space heading back to New Brunswick Station, another bad choice. Ah, there—twenty-six hours to the departure of the *Alpha Star,* a passenger transport heading to Artreal. It was a risk, but Pallas did want one more excursion to the casino before Oriah left.

Three hours into her play, a pleasantly familiar baritone voice from behind her said, "Good evening."

"Hello, Tanik," she said without looking. "A moment, please."

"Of course," and he stepped back as she finished the draw hand she was playing. Laying down a royal flush in clubs, she smiled as she raked the pile of chips into her sequined bag.

"Work or pleasure?" she asked, turning and sliding off the stool.

He smiled, taking her hand to kiss it. "Pure pleasure," he said. "I was hoping you'd join me for dinner."

"A delightful idea." The chance to spend her last few hours here with Tanik pleased her more than she wanted to admit.

The erotic pull of one telepath toward another could be extraordinarily strong. Something inside you recognized a kindred mind. Maybe it was natural selection, the telepath gene exerting the desire to increase the chance of telepathic offspring. Oriah had run into it before but never this intense. Tanik dangerously attracted and aroused her. She rarely indulged her physical desires and never while in the middle of the game. Now, when she knew she was leaving in a few hours, Oriah found her body was having a hard time listening to the admonishments of her common sense. In fact, said body was strongly urging her to chuck caution out the nearest airlock.

Dinner over, they were sharing an exquisite chocolate concoction drizzled with a sauce of some unpronounceable berry native to Sector IV. Even with her barriers in place, Oriah could sense Tanik's genuine affection for her. Did he feel the same pull she did? Did he yet suspect her gifts but willingly overlooked it? Oh, how she could lose herself in those beautiful sapphire eyes.

"You're staring at me," he said.

"So I am," she mused. "Such a lovely pastime to have." His cheeks colored slightly.

"And what might you be thinking?"

That you can't know this will be our last encounter; or how desperately I want you to be the good man you seem to be.

"That you are a puzzle, Tanik Sanovic," she ventured, taking the chance to find out. "I have run across many TSS agents in my line of work. They have all been . . . unpleasant, enjoying their work far too much, some sadistically so. But not you. You have an air of someone who is not doing the work he wishes to be doing."

Tanik looked down for a moment.

"No," he said quietly, "it is not my job of choice. But I do what is required in my contract."

"Catching cheaters?"

"Mostly. Sometimes conflict resolution. I am allowed to use my gifts to calm agitated patrons to prevent harm to others."

"Sounds like a tight leash. I have heard of this registry. I don't think I like it. But if this isn't what you want to be doing, why do it?"

He shrugged, then looked away at a memory. They were both teetering on the knife edge of trust. He looked into her eyes then, taking the first leap of faith.

"To keep my cousin from getting spaced," he said. "He was just a kid, his gift had just manifested, he didn't know what he was doing. When I arrived, they were threatening to put him out the airlock. I repaid the casino, went broke doing so, sent Ches home, then agreed to a five-year contract with the bureau as a TSS agent. Three hundred forty-nine days until it's up and all the fees are paid off."

Oriah knew it was truth and smiled.

"Sacrificing for family can be hard," she said, "but it is worth it." He smiled back, clearly relieved.

"So, in less than a year you will be free. What then?"

"Will you think less of me if I say politics?"

"No," she answered, suddenly serious. "I might even think more, depending on why."

"Because of what I've seen working

here. The power of the gaming lobby is obscene. The Bureau's inconsistency—there's corruption that needs to be exposed. The fear the Purity League is spreading," Oriah shuddered at the mention of the militant group, "and the way the BAXers are treated on every station is appalling." He had grown more animated as he talked, revealing this was his passion. "I just want to help make things better."

She raised her glass to him. "You have my vote."

"I'll hold you to that," and he clinked his glass to hers. There was a tension released between them.

"Have you been to the observation deck yet?" he asked.

"No, is it worth seeing?"

"Oh yes! Force fields let you walk as though suspended, surrounded by stars. Would you like to go?"

"It sounds wonderful! Let me just freshen up first."

She was nearing the lavatory, elated to find that he was the type of man she'd hoped he was. The rage behind her registered a moment too late. The prick of a needle, and her senses began to fog.

Tanik! Her mind screamed, all her barriers dropped in the only cry for help she could manage as Andy slipped an arm under her, half carrying her toward the service lift as the world spun to blackness.

Oriah woke slowly, the after effects of the drug making her groggy. She sat on the floor of a small room, leaning against one bare metal wall. The room was no more than a meter and a half wide, and maybe twice that long. A storage compartment. Her hands were tied with wire to an eye bolt in the wall next to her head. Her vision cleared, but her mind didn't. There was an odd buzzing she couldn't shake. Then she saw the small white device sitting near the door—a dampener.

He knew she was a telepath.

The dampener's frequency made concentration difficult, like a thousand tiny needles poking her brain. But how had someone like Andy gotten hold of a dampener? They were experimental technology, and as far as she knew, only the military and the bureau had access to them.

She had no way of knowing if Tanik had heard her mental call for help. And with the dampener, he wouldn't be able to find her telepathically. There had to be a way to get past the mind-numbing device.

The door opened, and Andy walked in, an ugly smirk on his face. He started pacing in front of her, flipping a knife casually in his right hand.

"You cost me a lot, bitch," he spat. "Now I'm locked out and for what? BAXer scum we're better off without."

Of course, Oriah thought, he was selling drugs he stole from the med bay.

"But you'll make up for it. The League'll pay me plenty for bringing them a telepath. And since you're a rogue, no one will miss you."

Only decades of practice kept the panic gripping Oriah's stomach from showing on her face. "You're insane, Andy," she said. "You got yourself fired."

"You did something to me!" He screamed. "I couldn't stop myself!" His pacing brought him closer. If she could use his anger and confidence in the dampener against him, make him careless, she might have a chance.

"They do say the truth will set you free," she said blandly.

"Not you," he sneered. "The truth will get you dissected. The League is going to find a way to prevent freaks like you ever being born."

He wanted her scared and upset, so she gave him calm boredom.

"I should have known you were one of *those*," she said, rolling her eyes then studying broken fingernail on her tied hands. "Bunch of ignorant bigots who think way too much of themselves." Telepathy wasn't the only way to push someone like Andy. When she looked back at him, her smile was condescending. "Then again, I suppose stupidity becomes you."

"We are the saviors of humanity! We will burn away what is impure and show the way for the worthy," he spouted the group's doctrine with practiced zealotry, and the knife stopped flipping. "You know, they said this only needed to be on the first setting, but you look way too comfortable. Let's try the tenth."

He used the tip of the blade to crank up the dampener, and Oriah cried out involuntarily as the buzzing pins turned to knives inside her skull.

"That's more like it," he said. "Not so smug now, are you? How do like the migraine?" He taunted her as he came closer. "I'm sure they won't mind if I take a souvenir. Lock of hair? Maybe a finger?"

Her foot shot out, the spiked heel of her shoe going deep into his left shin. The knife dropped as he howled, fell backward and knocked into the dampener, which hit the wall, bounced and rolled toward Oriah. She struggled to pull herself up, dizzy from the pain. She stretched her leg out and caught the cursed device with her foot bringing it closer as Andy started pulling himself up. Then she kicked hard and it hit the wall, the impact cracking the case. The cessation of pain left her numb and panting, slumped against the wall.

Andy limped toward her, the hole in his leg pouring blood. He grabbed the knife from the floor in a white knuckled fist, his face a murderous mask.

"They like it better if you're alive, but a corpse will do just fine," he growled.

He grabbed her hair and pulled her head back, knife raised. Her mind finally cleared enough to stop knife as he brought it down. It barely missed her as Andy doubled over and the knife clattered to the floor.

Hatred warred with fear in his eyes. Scorching rage, bitter revulsion, and abject terror washed over Oriah. Her eyes blurred with tears, the aftermath of the dampener leaving her too weak to risk walling out the onslaught.

"Go ahead," he spat. "Kill me. I know you can. That's what you people do."

He was right, she could, and it stung that she contemplated it for even a nanosecond. "No," she said simply. There was really nothing more to say, even if she'd had the strength. There was no reasoning with hysteria.

It took every ounce of will she had to keep Andy immobile. She couldn't even call to Tanik, only hope he sensed her before the effort became too much and she collapsed.

Her vision was starting to tunnel by the time the door burst open and Tanik rushed in.

"Pallas!"

"He's League," she managed, not taking her concentration from Andy until Tanik pulled out restraints and secured him. Then Oriah fell back against the wall, sliding slowly down to the floor again. Tanik untied her hands, and she fell into his arms, her tears spilling freely, drinking in the sweetness of his relief and affection, letting it crash over her in waves to drown out the aftertaste of Andy in her mind.

Tanik held her as she recovered her senses. "Are you all right?" he asked as Oriah pulled reluctantly from his arms to lean against the wall and massage her wrists.

"I will be," she said, nodding, then pointed to the remains of the dampener. "How did someone like him get hold of one of those?"

"I don't know," he said and walked over to Andy, "but I intend to find out."

"I won't tell you anything. You are an abomination of nature, and you will be purged!"

"Maybe," Tanik said calmly. He touched Andy's forehead and the man fell unconscious. "But not today."

Tanik picked up the pieces of the device in one hand, then held the other out for Oriah.

"I'll have regular security pick him up on kidnaping charges. The security feed near the lavatory clearly shows him injecting you." He shook his head. "I'll never say there's too many cameras again. Add that to the stash of drugs we found in his residence, and he'll be away for a very long time." He looked at the dampener pieces. "*This* I will hang on to for awhile."

Oriah stood over Andy, looking down at him.

"He expected me to kill him. He's terrified of us. They all are, the League, I wasn't even human to him." The bitterness she'd absorbed was hard to stomach. She'd just discovered one could get an overdose of emotions.

Oriah closed her eyes and reached into Andy's unconscious mind, carefully blocking his memory of what she was; then she looked at Tanik.

"It's your choice. You can restore the memory if you want." He nodded, appreciating the option, even if he had no intention of using it.

Back in Pallas's suite, Oriah walked to the sidebar and poured brandy for both of them, not bothering with the neutralizer. They sat on the sofa facing each other.

"You know, I suspected you were a rogue the day we met, but I have so wanted it not to be true."

Oriah shook her head, raising an eyebrow.

"No, you wanted it to be true, you just wanted it not to matter." All pretense was gone. "It isn't illegal to be an unregistered telepath." She took a sip of the brandy. "Not yet, anyway."

"But it is illegal for a telepath to gamble."

"Unless you gamble for the casino? I know you don't, but it is perfectly legal for a casino to hire a telepath to gamble for the house. Besides, it all depends on whether you follow the letter of the law or the intent."

"Meaning?"

"The intent of the law is to save casinos from excessive cheating and keep their customers from being unfairly taken advantage of, except by the casino itself. I use my talents—all my talents—to my advantage, yes, but I don't use my gifts to cheat. I am, telepath or not, a very good *professional* gambler. My parents were legendary, and they taught me well. Besides, the casino benefits from my presence. I make people feel good, Tanik. People who feel good and are enjoying themselves are better for the casino."

He gave her a skeptical look

"Check the casino's profits," and she raised her glass to him then took another sip, rather enjoying the buzz of the alcohol. "They went up every hour I was in there, and down when I wasn't. I'm better for the casino than most of their dealers."

"I doubt that would hold up in court." His tone was sardonic and she shrugged, knowing he wasn't planning on turning her in. "I'm not supposed to let you leave here with your winnings," he said and she laughed.

"I rarely leave with much more than I arrived with," she said and reached up to brush a stray lock of hair from his face, then she opened her memories of the excursions to the BAX7 and BAX8 slums. Tanik saw Dina and little Andria, Tony and all the others until he shook his head in dismay.

"A regular Lady Robin Hood," he chuckled, "you keep surprising me."

"Good," she said sliding close to him, not caring if the alcohol was affecting her judgment. She reached her hand up to caress the back of his neck, entwining her fingers in his hair and pulling his mouth to hers. Then reached out, mind to mind, all barriers down, offering him the most intimate connection one human can have with another—the total sharing of consciousness. There was no resistance, for he had wanted this as much as she did. By the time their bodies were as joined as their minds, they knew every fear and joy, sorrow and celebration each had experienced.

"Oriah," he whispered as they lay entwined on her bed, enjoying the afterglow, "what a beautiful name."

"Thank you. I hear it so rarely."

"You could hear it more often if you stopped running."

"Your word, not mine. I enjoy playing my game. And traveling is not running."

"But you can't be yourself."

"I am always myself. I just

concentrate on different aspects of myself. The next time I'm here, I may be Yasimi or Ingrid or Candice, but I will also be Oriah. We are all the same person."

"If you ever return to this station—and I do hope you will return—I won't be able to let you in the casino."

This brought a chuckle. "If you're here. You only have a year left. That's a year of planning before you run for the Sol Senate."

Tanik propped himself up on one elbow, looking down at her. "You're serious. One doesn't usually *start* one's political career with the Senate."

She smiled. "So be the first. I think Senator Tanik Sanovic has a nice ring to it, don't you?"

They remained lightly linked, and he saw her imagine his whole campaign.

"You said you wanted to change things. I think you could succeed. You've been on the inside, so you have credibility. You're educated, articulate," then she winked, adding "and you look smashing in a tuxedo." She could feel the wheels begin to turn in the back of his mind.

She kissed him, muddling his thoughts.

Think about it—tomorrow.

The *Alpha Star* pulled away from Castille Station. On the portage deck a hundred desperate, agitated people were all hoping that the next station would be the place to find work or freedom or escape from whatever trouble they were fleeing.

Oriah sat in an alcove drinking in the bittersweet emotions, then sending back to these weary, forgotten people a soothing sense of calm, quiet peace. The tang of fear eased. It was a full week to Artréal Station, and they would experience the disorientation of jumping three times. If people began the trip unnerved, patience would be impossible toward the end. Oriah pulled in and sent one last time then closed off her mind.

Castille would be a station to remember. She hadn't expected Tanik. Such a rare and special man. Oriah closed her eyes, smiling at the memory of Tanik's mind and body entwined with hers. She would have to start banking more of her winnings if she wanted to be one of the financial backers for his senate campaign.

One couldn't get rid of entrenched prejudice and fear overnight, and Oriah knew she couldn't change the galaxy single-handedly, but she did try to throw stones in the pond. Normals like Dina and Andria, learning one need not be afraid of the gifted, were little stones. The ripple was the story they would pass along to others. Then there was Tanik, inspired to work for change from within the power structures. Helping him would be a boulder added to her stones. With enough thrown into the still pond of political complacency, the ripples would eventually become waves, and waves had the power to change everything.

FLASH
by
Cat Greenberg

*This was originally written for a
microfiction contest. The challenge was
to write a story in 100 words or less. It
seemed a fitting end to this anthology.*

Her death was glorious. As a sliver of
waning moon shed insignificant light,
the flames of her funeral pyre leapt and
pirouetted in the darkness, a wild dance
of divine agony until her essence lay still
and quiet.

Slowly came the regrowth of
heart and bone, sinew and skin, then
glistening feathers of gold and black.
She stretched new wings, screeching in
triumph. With one powerful flap, the ash
of her old life fell away, scattering in the
breeze as the Phoenix soared into her
brilliant new life.

Made in the USA
Monee, IL
21 October 2021

80288253R10173